Zola

D E McCluskey

D E McCluskey

ZOLA

Copyright © 2021 by D E McCluskey

Dammaged Production

www.dammaged.com

Zola

For Lisa Lee Tone...

A long-suffering editor, who loves extreme horror

but struggled to get through my children's book

on seagulls.

I wrote this one especially for you. Enjoy!

D E McCluskey

Zola

Part One:

Andrea

1.

ANTHONY NAMED THEIR child.

It was a joke.

It was another in a long line of jokes, with her as the punchline. It was one of many over the years, but this one might have been the cruellest.

Just like the bruises to her body and face, the jokes had started early on in their relationship. After the honeymoon period of flowers, perfume, wild nights out, and even wilder nights in, it was in the bedroom where the real Anthony Zola revealed himself. They had tied the knot quickly and moved into their very own home. That was when Anthony Zola, the version who had been patiently waiting in the wings, salivating, ready to pounce and attack at a moment's provocation, showed himself.

It was when the nervous laughs and the '*Come on Andrea, pick yourself up. You know I didn't mean it,*' and the '*If you tell anyone, I'll fucking kill you,*' began.

It had always been her fault.

The little digs, the jokes at her expense whenever they were in company. The fake excuses when he didn't come home for days, when she knew he'd gotten a bonus from work, or earned a few extra bucks on the side.

To his credit, he was a hard worker. To his many discredits, he was also a hard drinker, and an even harder hitter.

His ugly wit usually came to the fore when he'd been drinking, and he was *usually* drinking. But, when he insisted on naming their child, it felt like the final insult, a nail in Andrea's coffin.

He'd tried to explain why he did it. 'It'll make him tough,' he insisted. 'You know, like in that song. The one where the kid has a girl's name. Sue or Sandra or some shit.'

But Andrea knew the truth.

It was to ridicule her, to embarrass her in front of friends, to push them further from the world, to isolate her.

To her shame, she allowed it to happen.

When the boy was born, her mother and father, her sister, cousins, and friends had all flocked to her. But her awkwardness, and coldness had pushed them away, one by one. All at the behest of her controlling husband.

When they asked what the boy's name was, she knew they'd laugh, she knew they'd talk about her behind her back. There would be talk about how she'd changed, how she'd let Anthony control her.

And all this talk would be correct, all part of his plan.

She hated the boy's name.

Anthony had been drunk, laughing when he announced what it was to be. She remembered bringing the child home, wrapped in a bright yellow blanket. It had been the only thing she'd been allowed to buy new. Everything else had been worn or ripped, hand-me-downs from people she didn't know, purchases from Goodwill shops. 'I'm not spending the money I've worked these fingers to the bone for, just to buy clothes for some snot nosed little brat,' was just one of his favourite rants. 'He'll be grown out of them in a week, and what a load of wasted cash that'll have been.'

She had been so embarrassed about the situation that when they had him Christened, she never asked anyone to come. The only people present were a few of Anthony's friends. When they went to celebrate afterwards, she was sent home to tend to the child.

Anthony didn't come home for three days.

She hadn't slept a wink in all that time, worrying that something had happened to him, fretting how she, and her child, would survive without a man in their lives. Fortunately, or maybe unfortunately, nothing bad had happened. He had just been engaging in a three-day binge, blowing all their money on drink and God only knew what else.

When he eventually came home, stinking of alcohol, perfume, and sweat, she found she didn't care where he'd been. All she cared about was her boy and him having a father around to support him, to protect him, to teach him the ways of the world.

It made her sad that he'd have to go through the whole of his life with such a ridiculous name. But she was sure Anthony was correct. It would toughen the boy towards the cruel world waiting for him.

~~~~

One of Andrea's big loves was cheese.

It had always been her favourite snack, ever since she was a child.

When they were courting, Anthony would tease her about how much of it she ate. 'Hell, Andrea. You eat so much cheese, it's my reckoning you'll turn into a block one of these days.' He would laugh at this joke, and she would too. After all, it was only a small ribbing, just a little something that was part of his personality. The personality she was falling head over heels in love with.

Only the jokes never stopped.

In fact, they got worse, meaner, especially when she started gaining weight, not long after the wedding. It was the same old joke, only the cheese was sometimes replaced by lard. 'You're gonna end up looking like a tub of lard,' he'd sneer. 'I isn't putting my dick into a bucket of grease.'

He'd laugh, as if it were the funniest thing he'd ever heard in his life. It wasn't funny. It was cruel, it was hurtful, and it sent Andrea into a downward cycle.

She knew she was a cliché.

She ate because she was unhappy, and she was unhappy because she ate.

Some joke, huh? She would ask herself.

However, when it came to *putting his dick in a bucket of grease,* his morals were not so upstanding when he'd been drinking. He was more than happy to slip his dingus into her greasy bucket then. He also had a penchant to be a little too free with his fists too. It had started innocently, just a little hair pulling during sex, which she found she didn't mind, it excited her a little. However, by the time she found out she was pregnant, the playfulness had been replaced by slapping, choking, and the occasional punch.

That, she did mind.

She had read that it was normal, that some women even liked it. She was convinced the books and magazines stating this had been secretly written by men, because she didn't find anything enjoyable about being slapped, punched, or strangled, during sex or not.

Getting pregnant had been the best thing that had happened to her, as Anthony's sex drive, towards her at least, depleted. She was convinced he was sticking his dingus into someone else's grease bucket, and even though it made her sad, she found she had no problem with it.

If he's sticking it into someone else, at least he's leaving me alone.

He never came near her for almost the whole term, but the jibes continued, as did the beatings.

One of the issues she experienced, which only exacerbated her situation, were her wild pregnancy cravings. She loved cheese, and probably did eat a little more than she should, but it seemed her baby shared her love of it too.

She would wake in the middle of the night—Anthony snoring drunkenly beside her, or not there at all—with the child nestling in her belly, crying out for a little something.

That little something was cheese.

The smellier the cheese, the better.

The weight piled on during pregnancy. She hoped it was just childbearing weight, that it would fall off when the child came. However, she knew, deep down, in her thickening chest, it was here to stay.

When the boy was born, Anthony was present. He played the part of the doting father and the caring husband to aplomb. He held her hand, he mopped her brow, he bought her flowers.

But she knew it was all an act.

The act was exposed for the sham it was once the baby was born.

The child came with jaundice. Yellow skin and yellow eyes. Anthony was passed the child once he'd been smacked on the behind to clear his tubes and the crying had started. He told Andrea later that the name for the child came to him in a flash of inspiration. 'I was holding the little yellow *bastard* in my arms,' he told her. 'He was all veiny and yellow with the jaundice, that the name kind of popped into my head.'

Whenever he told this tale, and he told it many times, usually during a bleeding nose or nursing a bruise, she hated him. The beatings no longer bothered her, his running around with other women, his drunken slovenly behaviour, none of it bothered her; she had grown accustomed to them. But what he'd done to her son she would never forgive.

It all began with the name.

It was a shame she would bear for the rest of her life.

The name Anthony gave their child, their son, was Gordon.

His name was Gordon Zola!

Zola

2.

THE JOKES CONTINUED, especially after the baby weight failed to shed like her friends, her family, and the magazines she read had told her it would. Her hips were wider, her breasts were in serious danger of losing their battle with gravity, and her face still carried the chubbiness of pregnancy. She felt ugly, and this feeling was exasperated almost every single day, when she was informed, by him, that she was every bit as bad as she felt. She no longer wanted to leave the house and would, only for essential shopping; cleaning products, hygiene products, the products that Gordon needed, and of course, for cheese.

As her friends began to fall by the wayside, mainly due to her inability to connect with anyone other than her boy, and her family gave up on her, after she refused to leave the *horrible bastard* she was married to, a dependency was born, a dependency on two products only.

The first was the gin to get her through the physical violence bestowed upon her, both sexual and casual.

The second was cheese. Her comfort food.

She filled the cupboards with them both.

They cured her hangovers in the morning. They picked her up in the afternoons. If she felt sick, she would eat the cheese and drink the gin, it always made her feel better. When she got nervous, usually at the thought of Anthony coming home late from work, knowing he'd been drinking, she would repeat the cycle.

Her life had hit rock bottom, and the sad part of it all was that she knew it. But at least she had Gordon. He would get her through the rough days, and the nights too. She would fall asleep drunk, her face and lower regions throbbing from the beating they'd endured, her head throbbing from the gin she'd drunk to get her through the ordeal, stinking of cheese, but always with a smile on her face. The thought of seeing her boy's beautiful, smiles in the morning made her happy. It was her reason to get up in the mornings.

Life continued this way for the best part, or maybe the worst parts, of seven years. By this time, she had no one left in her life. Her small support circle of friends and family were long gone. She was closing in on two hundred and ten pounds, her hair was mostly grey, and she looked at least twenty years older than her twenty-eight trips around the sun.

Gordon, however, was a healthy, bouncy, attentive, handsome, bright boy.

In her eyes at least.

In truth, he was already overweight. He was a sullen and withdrawn child. He could only speak a few words, he couldn't read, and other than to go to the doctor or to go to the shops for gin and cheese, he never left the house.

All of his life, his father had mostly ignored him. However, since his seventh birthday, he had suddenly become the apple of daddy's eye.

Andrea hated the attention Anthony bestowed upon him.

It began as overfriendliness. Anthony started taking him out mostly to the park or for longs walks. 'Got to get some of this baby weight off him,' he'd say. 'You might want to think about doing the same,' he'd laugh.

The same old jokes she'd heard for years.

To Andrea, it didn't sit right. Why, after all this time of ignoring the boy, would he now be interested in his weight? She didn't want to dwell on it too much, *after all*, she told herself, *a boy needs a father to show him right from wrong.*

Life kind of started to become bearable for her. Gordon seemed happier than she he'd ever been, and Anthony changed too. Not in the bedroom, or in any of the other unsavoury aspects of his life, but he became less inclined to use his fists.

He began taking the boy out with him. Not only for walks but to meet his friends. Gordon was more than happy to go. He told his mother that when they went to the bars, there were other kids there and that he'd made friends. 'There are also other men, daddy's friends,' he told her. 'They're all really nice to me. They always give me sweets, and money.'

His face had beamed so bright when he mentioned he had friends, that she thought her heart might literally burst with joy.

Her little boy, her *only* reason for living, was finally happy.

Then came the extra money. At first, it was only a few dollars here, and a few there. She suspected Anthony was drinking the rest or spending it on the filthy whores she knew he frequented. But the extra came in handy. They could finally start making plans.

That first night, when Anthony had come home stinking of beer, cigarettes, and another woman's perfume, as was the norm, she didn't care. All she cared about was the stack of dollar bills he placed on the table.

'Where did they come from?' she asked, her eyes flicking towards Gordon, his bulk sat on the floor, playing with the new toys his father had bought.

'Why ask?' he asked, shaking his head. 'It's yours. You can use it to freshen this place up.'

She picked up the stack and counted it.

Fifty dollars.

It had been a long time since she'd seen fifty dollars. *If ever,* she thought.

'There's more where that came from too,' he said out of the side of his mouth, lighting a cigarette. She noted it was from a new, metal cigarette lighter with his name engraved on the side. Absently, she wondered where he'd gotten it, then remembered that she didn't care.

She took the money and put it in a place where she knew he would never look, if and when he changed his mind and demanded it back.

It was in her personal hygiene box.

~~~~

A few weeks later, the box was heavier. In fact, it was almost bursting. She had counted the bills the night before and was pleased to find that the amount had grown to just shy of four hundred dollars.

An absolute fortune.

Feeling better than she had in a long while, she dared a quick peep into the full-length mirror in the bedroom. Her good mood ebbed almost as quickly as it had flowed when she gazed upon herself. *How have I let herself go so much*, she thought. The two-hundred-pound mark had been left behind a long time ago.

She studied her hair, her face, her life. She cringed, internally as much as she did externally.

What must Gordon think every time he looks at his Mommy?

She went straight downstairs, into the kitchen. She opened the cupboards, the ones filled with cheeses and bottles of gin, and there and then, decided. She would rid herself of everything that was making her sad, that was keeping her down. From now on, she would begin to look after herself, to take pride in her appearance, if not for her own self-esteem, then she'd do it for Gordon.

She removed the many packages of cheese; some of them were out of date and had gone hard, but she'd never cared much about that, 'We can make fondue,' she'd say to Gordon, but mostly to herself. Not today, though. Today everything was going into the bin. The cheese, the empty bottles (after she had poured the gin down the sink), everything was going.

Her life was about to change.

Once she tied the bin bags and dumped them into the trash, she sighed, and by the time she flopped into her favourite seat, she was

15

grinning. The smile felt good on her face. She tried to remember when she had last had one that wasn't about something Gordan had done and couldn't remember.

This made her grin even more.

Maybe I'll ring Chrissy, she thought. Chrissy was her sister. They hadn't talked in an age. *Too long,* she thought nodding.

She dipped into the money box and counted a hundred dollars. Slipping it into her purse, she took herself off into town. She needed new clothes, as did Gordon.

For the first time, in a long time, there was a song in her heart.

~~~~

It was a few weeks later, with another six hundred dollars in the box, that the change in Gordon's behaviour became noticeable.

It was another few weeks after that, with a further thousand dollars in the box, that she suddenly found herself a widow, and a single parent.

Zola

3.

THE WEIGHT LOSS had gone well. She had been eating healthy, a balanced diet of meat, fish, vegetables, and fruits adorned the cupboards and refrigerator. Some of her old clothes, if she could even call them that— *rags would be more appropriate,* she thought with a grin—no longer fitted her, and new dresses, skirts and tops, that complimented her new slim-line figure, replaced them.

She was back to way under the two hundred pound mark for the first time in years and her outlook on life was the most optimistic she'd felt in years.

Life was beginning to open up to her again. She was stronger, fitter, healthier than she'd ever been. She was back in touch with her sister, and even had plans to meet up with her that weekend. She'd held her breath when picking up the phone to make *that* call. She needn't have worried as the sisters sat and conducted the longest conversation they'd had in probably five, maybe even six years.

Everything felt as if it were back on track.

Thankfully, Anthony had lost all interest in her, and with his loss of libido came a reprieve from the beatings.

Everything was coming up rosy.

~~~~

It was a Tuesday.

She remembered that fact clearly.

Anthony had been out with Gordon and their friends. She was counting the money in the box, daydreaming about how much more she would need before she could afford to leave this life, take her son, and reconnect with friends and family.

She put the money back into the box when the front door slammed closed. Her heart plummeted into her stomach causing everything inside it to churn. This was nothing new, it happened every time *he* came home.

Stop allowing him into your head, she chastised herself.

She descended the stairs to greet him, the ugly feelings she'd become accustomed to, but hadn't felt in a few weeks, came flooding back for some reason. It was in the flipping of her stomach, the feeling like she needed to go to the toilet, the tingling in her arms and her fingers. Anthony was kneeling in front of the boy, wiping his little face. It took her a moment to realise Gordon had a black eye and it looked like there'd been a bloody nose too.

Like an eighteen-wheel truck in the fast lane of the highway, her old life slammed into her, hitting her full in the face. She reeled backwards, grabbing the banister to stop from falling down the steps.

The realisation that over the last few months, the good times she'd experienced had been nothing but a brief oasis in the ugly, barren desert of her life, struck. It struck hard. She should have known, sooner or later, that she'd be forced to leave the table of plenty, and face the stark reality of the desolate, dunes before her.

They stretched out as far as her eyes could see.

It took her a moment to build enough breath in her lungs. When she was physically able to speak, her voice was thin, reedy. She hated herself for that show of weakness, but self-loathing, for her was like taxes, it was inevitable. 'Who-what happened?'

Before she knew it, she was down the stairs, snatching the chubby seven-year-old from his father. Anthony was grinning; there was something in his eyes, something cold, menacing that scared her, worse than she'd ever been scared before.

It might have been what real fear felt like.

'Ah, it's nothing he won't shake off,' Anthony said with a chuckle. 'He had a bit of a scuffle with one of the other boys, that's all. Nothing earth shattering. The boy's tough, he'll get over it.'

Anthony took the boy back from his mother's arms, where his arms were wrapped around her girth, and his head was buried into her stomach. 'Come on, Gordy. Go to your room. Me and your mother have some things we need to discuss,' he sang almost playfully.

With a bowed head, Gordon allowed himself to be prised from his mother's sanctuary, but his wide, moist eyes never once left hers.

When he was gone and the door to his room had closed, Anthony's turned his gaze on her. He was nodding as she felt his eyes all over her new figure. They lingered on her breasts.

She folded her arms.

'Well, you seem to be looking better these days,' he slurred.

It was the first time she noticed the familiar warm stink of alcohol on his breath. For some reason she couldn't pinpoint, it scared her more than it ever had before.

She could feel his pink eyes penetrating places she would never want them to go again, ever. Something told her she would be submitting to his will tonight, either that or endure a beating. Although she knew the two were never, really mutually exclusive.

'Come here, woman,' he ordered. 'I've got something for you.'

'Not now, Anthony. Gordon's upset …'

He removed a large wad of dollars from the inside pocket of his jacket.

He was still grinning.

Her brow creased. 'What's that?' she whispered, not quite able to think straight.

'This is what you could call a bonus,' he said with another laugh. 'Seven hundred bucks, and it's all for you.'

And how much was just for you? she thought.

'But you need get over here and earn it,' he ordered with a sneer.

She hated him at that moment.

'Come on, Anthony, not tonight. Gordon's upset—'

Zola

'Yes, fucking tonight,' he hissed. She flinched as his foul smelling spittle landed on her face. 'Gordon's upset? Don't you think I'm upset?' he snapped. 'Do you think I enjoyed watching that fat ass little faggot get a beating from a kid younger than him, and half his size? Don't you think I need a little sugar to make that medicine go down?'

His top lip was furled, and it was twitching. She could read it; and recognised it wasn't a good sign. She knew what it meant. She knew she would have a matching eye with Gordon by the morning. She didn't want to, but for the sake of Gordon, and she was almost ashamed to admit it, the money Anthony had been filling her hygiene box with, she knew she would be taking the punishment tonight.

'That's right,' he whispered as he pulled her closer. 'Give daddy what he needs.'

The fact he called himself *daddy* turned her stomach.

However, when he grabbed her by her recently coloured hair, wrapping it around his hand and pulling her closer towards his fist, towards his stinking mouth, and his stinking penis—a penis she knew would be venturing into places penises were not supposed to go … she was revolted even more.

~~~~

Luckily, it was not a prolonged ordeal.

Anthony had always been firmly in the camp of not caring if the woman was as sexually satisfied as he was. It was one of the reasons—but not the only one, for sure—why she didn't care about his infidelities.

21

To be honest, she pitied the women he frequented.

Her cheek was sore, as was her ass.

He penetrated her in ways she knew were not legal, especially in the eyes of God. He also punched her, scratched her, spat on her, and called her names, the like she'd never heard before and hoped never to again.

But thankfully, he had never been one for maintaining his libido.

Once he'd released, wherever he decided that was to be, she knew he would be asleep within minutes.

Tonight was no different.

Leaning over, she checked on him. Satisfied he was asleep, she winced as she levered herself off the bed. He had been rough tonight, but she'd been through worse.

She wanted to put the money in the box with the rest of it without him getting any knowledge of it, she knew that if he knew where it was, he'd spend it.

The room was dark, but she didn't want to put a light on, in case it woke Anthony, and his wicked, but shitty libido.

She picked up her clothes and dragged them to the door, intending to go through them on the landing, when a noise took her breath away. It was only a small sound, but it's meaning was mighty. It was a sound she hadn't heard in a long time.

Suddenly she was eight years of age, standing at the door to her bedroom and bursting to go to the toilet, but not wanting to as she thought she had just heard a noise in the big house.

She stopped what she was doing, glad of the camouflage of the dark, and cocked her head. The sound was gone now, and she quizzed herself on if she'd even heard it at all.

Her focus returned to getting to the landing, and getting the money into her box, when it came again.

She had been right about it, although she wished she hadn't.

Dropping the trousers she was investigating, she looked towards the dim light that was coming from the frame of the closed bedroom door.

When the noise came for a third time, it brought with it a throb. It was in her head, it was in her chest, it was everywhere. Her throat was dry, her legs felt like jelly, and more than a twinge of nausea accompanied it.

As her head spun, she began a mantra in her head. *Something's not right,* she thought. *Something's not right, something's not right.* Then there was one final, doomsday thought that blew everything she was feeling, all the fear, all her anxiety, all her trepidation. It was a simple, but powerful thought.

Everything changes tonight.

The calm that thought brought with it shocked her. *Is that a premonition?*

It turned out, it was!

The noise was constant now, and there was no way she could deny it.

It was a sob.

At first, she wanted to dismiss it, only because it had been so long since she'd heard anything like it coming from someone else other than herself. But its persistence told her she couldn't dismiss it, not anymore.

With a moist hand, she reached for the door handle. A part of her didn't want to turn it. A part of her, maybe the part that had given her the premonition moments ago, knew that what lay beyond the bedroom door was madness. A torment, a blackness she might fall into and never, ever escape. However, she knew she was going to turn the handle, abyss, or no abyss. Her boy was out there, lost in that darkness, and he needed her. Sparing a glance back at the piece of shit snoring in their bed, she powered on, headlong into the velvety obsidian, ready for whatever was waiting for her.

Or at least that was what she thought.

The sob *was* coming from Gordon's room. She held her breath and knocked lightly before pushing the door open.

'Hey, baby …' she whispered.

The sobbing stopped instantly.

'Gordon, are you OK?' she asked. Her heart was pounding in her ears so loud that it might have drowned out any words of response. However, the silence was deafening. 'Gordon, it's Mom. Are you OK?'

There was just one word as an answer.

The silence, the darkness, everything she had been building in her life was shattered with that one, single word.

It was a word she had *loved* hearing just a few short years ago. But hearing it now broke her. Her heart snapped in her chest, and her sanity exploded, leaving glassy slivers shattered in her head.

'Mommy?' the small voice whispered. It was the scared voice of a child, yet it was filled with age, with dread, with knowledge of things a seven, nearly eight-year-old boy should never, ever know.

She reached for the light switch. Once again, part of her hoped she couldn't, or wouldn't, ever find it. But there it was, a cold plastic switch beneath her moist fingers.

She flicked it.

Gordon was sitting up in bed. His pyjamas—the ones with his favourite cartoons on them, a werewolf by the name of Fangface, who could turn simply by looking at a picture of a full moon—were bunched up around him. There was blood all over the covers.

A panic washed over her, and she bounded into the room. Other than his swollen eye and bruised nose, she couldn't find another wound on his body. And she looked, thoroughly, even though, he winced every time she moved him.

Then she saw where the blood was coming from.

Her eyes went fuzzy, just for a moment, as her brain battled to disguise what it was seeing. But there was no way it could ever disguise this.

The blood was all over his pyjama bottoms.

It was coming from the back.

At first, her brain was winning the fight for non-recognition, as she simply could not fathom what it was she was looking at. Then slowly, the horrific realisation dawned on her. Hadn't she bled from the exact same place the first few times he had taken *her* that way?

Her fear began to ebb.

The tidal waters of insanity were receding. The beach of madness was wiping itself clean of every bad thing that has washed up on its shore, just for the moment. She was working on a different plane now. She was a blank canvas ready to be filled with something else, something new. She knew it would be anger. A dangerous kind of wrath would soon be filling that void; but now, she was vanilla, cool headed, and living in the moment.

She looked at the pyjama bottoms. They were soiled, ruined. The stains were brown, and it was only then she noticed the odd smell. It was metallic copper mixed with faeces. It looked like dried blood, but from bitter experience, she knew. Many a night she had sat on the toilet, wiping the same stink from her until the early hours of the morning, listening to *that bastard,* snore as he slept the sleep of the just.

She knew there would be shit mixed in with the blood.

'Mommy?' he whispered again.

'I'm here, baby,' she soothed, surprised at how calm she sounded. 'I'm always here.'

'I'm scared, Mommy. My bottom hurts, it's all wet and it stings.' He was a petrified three-year-old, one who'd been scolded for doing something wrong. Her brain felt as if it were going to snap, and her reality would become askew. She would let that all happen later, right now she had to help her son through this.

'I've got something that'll stop the bleeding,' she soothed, leaving her hand to linger on his wet hair as she climbed off the bed. She reached behind her and grasped the door. She cursed the doorknob; it had been the entrance to this shitty alternate reality. Once again, she wished she hadn't wandered into this level of Hell, but she had, and she was stuck now, needing to work with the cards she'd been dealt.

'Don't leave,' he whimpered. His voice pathetic, frightened, hurt. He was damaged, and she knew it was down to her to fix him.

'I'll only be a moment, baby. You stay there. Don't you move a muscle. Mommy's coming right back.'

She left him sobbing in his own filth.

With every sigh, every shaky breath, a little bit of her, the old and newer Andrea, died. The reality of her life was cracking, peeling, falling away, but she had to be strong, for her son, and for herself. There was an unpleasant job ahead of her, *before the more important, and even more unpleasant one ahead of that,* she thought, surprised that the foamy tide of her wrath hadn't returned to the beach of tranquillity yet.

She retrieved what she needed and returned to Gordon's room to see he'd heeded her very words. He hadn't moved from his position in the corner of the room. 'OK, baby,' she soothed. 'This is going to be a little uncomfortable, but it's going to help. You need to trust me. Do you trust your momma?'

The boy nodded, his thick black hair flopping onto his wet face.

She smiled. It was warm, and nothing but unconditional. Her broken heart was just about ready to go all out to him. 'I need you to lie on your stomach, baby. It's going to sting, just a little bit, but I need you to be a big boy about it. Can you do that?'

The child, who was no longer innocent and, now that she thought about it, probably hadn't been for a long time, did as she asked. 'I don't want to go out with Daddy again,' he whispered. 'I don't like his friends.'

She ignored what he had just said, putting it to the back of her mind, for now. 'I just need to pull your jammies down a little. I'm going to clean you up and put something in there that will stop the bleeding. OK?'

The boy nodded, doing exactly what she asked. He lay on his stomach, allowing her to pull his bloody cheeks apart.

A thought occurred to her, and on the horizon of her beach there was just a hint of what was to come. It was a hellfire, but it wasn't here yet, it was still a way off.

How often has he been ordered to do that exact thing?

She hated herself for that thought but again, she would deal with that later, right now she was busy focusing her hatred on Anthony. It got her through this most difficult task.

There was blood all over his bottom. Her stomach tightened at seeing her own flesh and blood, the one person in this whole world who she loved more than life itself, in this state. But she had a job to do, and she would do it to the best of her abilities.

She wiped him, allowing for his flinches and whimpers at her touch. She battled her thoughts through teary eyes. His skin was bruised black and blue. There were red welts all over his flesh. As she continued to wipe, he continued to flinch, but he never once cried out until she pulled his cheeks gently apart.

Her mouth screwed into a tight hole, and she bit into her cheeks until she could taste blood. His anus was torn; it was where the blood was flowing from. Her fingers tingled as she soothed him, but she could feel the preliminary waves of wrath lapping at her beach. Her numbness was subsiding, and the rawness of the wounds, the physical ones on his body, not to mention the mental ones in his head, were exposed.

She continued to wipe the mix of blood and faeces away. There was very little else she could do.

He inhaled sharply at each dab.

'Not long now,' she whispered in a sing-song voice that she didn't know was for him, or her. Sniffing, she kept her tears at bay.

She knew they would come, they *would* come, along with the tsunami of rage threatening her horizon. It was also possible they may never stop. Either way, she would welcome them. They would make her feel human, unlike the robot she was now.

Her son's anus was torn. It was ripped badly.

She thought about that. *How did things get this far?*

It was worse than anything *that bastard* had ever inflicted on her. The ugly thoughts of Gordon being used, passed around by the *cunts* he called friends, made the wave she knew was coming double, maybe even triple in size. The fact that he may never recover from this dawned on her.

It might have been another premonition, but that was for the future.

She was having enough trouble dealing with the present.

'Did...' She swallowed her words in a sob she hadn't seen coming. 'Did Daddy do this to you?' she whispered into the stark light of the room. The not knowing if she wanted an answer hurt her more than the answer she anticipated. Not knowing would allow her to live the rest of her life in blissful ignorance. It was too late for that. That boat had sailed. It was a single sailor in a tiny yacht, heading out to face the mega tsunami that was coming to her shore.

She had to be ready to hear the truth.

However, she was wholly unprepared for the truth.

'Yes,' he whispered. 'Him and his friends.'

With a calm, sad smile on her lips, and cold, empty eyes, she ripped the packaging from the tampon she'd brought from the bathroom. 'This is going to be uncomfortable,' she whispered. 'It might hurt a little too.' *Although nowhere near as bad as you've been hurt before,* she thought, bitterly.

He moaned, crying out, just the once, as she slipped the cottonwool probe into a place tampons were not designed for. She then took a tub of white cream and gently slathered the ruined area around the protruding string.

When she was done and he was wearing a clean pair of pyjamas and there were fresh bed sheets on the bed, she cradled him in her arms, and sang a soothing lullaby, hoping it would lull him into something that resembled sleep.

Amazingly, it worked. In the comfort of her arms, the boy dozed.

She smiled and wiped away a single tear as she looked upon the love of her life. Everything was going to be so different when he awoke. The red danger flags were flapping on the beach of her mind.

The dangerous tide was coming in, and it was coming fast.

Zola

4.

GORDON EVENTUALLY FELL asleep, albeit a moody, dark version of sleep, but she could tell by the rapid movement of his eyes it was deep. The rhythmic rising and falling of his chest and the depth of his breathing told her he was out. *Poor little thing,* she thought, fixing his hair from his face. He looked almost peaceful, at something resembling rest. Her heart swelled with her love for him, but that swelling was only brief. The tide was about to break. She could feel a new swelling, one filled with anger, and rage. The unadulterated apocalyptic wrath she'd been harbouring was about to crash through.

She had heard about a *pink mist* descending over people who were as lost in ire as she was, but she had never thought she would physically see one, but she was seeing it now. Her world was bathed in a pink tinge that was offering her the clarity of what needed to be done.

A smile washed over her when she realised she didn't *have* to do what she had in mind, *but I fucking want to.*

She tucked the sleeping Gordon into his clean blankets and closed the door behind her, hiding him away from what was about to happen.

Her insides were churning. They were a turmoil of undulating molten lava. Externally, she had the appearance of being cool, calm even. Her hands were not shaking, she couldn't even feel the elevated beating of her heart, there was no throb in her head, no sheen of sweat on her body, and the tingling of her fingers had receded.

I'm cool, just like Fonzie. This thought made her smile.

Going downstairs, she entered the kitchen and gathered two items. She needed, *no*, she stopped herself mid thought. *These are items I want!* She *wanted* them for the job at hand. Her vision was not blurred, and best of all, she wasn't second guessing herself, telling herself this was *not* a good idea. She grinned as she thought about two cartoon versions of herself sitting on her shoulders. One was a devil, all dressed in red, complete with horns and a pitchfork. The other was an angel, dressed in white, with a halo and a harp.

'Do it ...' the devilish cartoon goaded her. 'Give that *cunt* everything that's coming to him.'

'Kill the pig-fucking twat,' the angelic version agreed. 'That dirty prick is nothing but shit on your shoe.'

She held the two objects before her and nodded her approval of them, then made her way back upstairs. She knew that when she came back down, she would be a completely different person.

She counted the steps. There were thirteen of them. The irony was not lost on her. *Unlucky for him,* she giggled.

The door to their bedroom was closed, but she could hear his snoring even through the thick wood. *Grunting like the pig he is.* For the first time, her stomach churned, not because of what she was about to do but because of the thought of him sleeping while her boy suffered. He had passed her son around, *his fucking son*, to be used, to be abused and fucked by sick perverts for financial gain. The thought sickened her, but it also buoyed her onwards. She gripped the door handle, turned it, and entered the darkness, a darkness she knew full well she might never escape from.

She welcomed it.

The stink of alcohol and farts assaulted her nose, but she battled through it. It wasn't like she hadn't slept through that stench before.

The *need* to do what she was about to do turned into a *wanting*.

'Anthony?' she whispered. 'Are you awake?'

The man, the stranger, the child rapist, the pimp in her bed mumbled something indecipherable and turned on his side, releasing a long, hissing expulsion of wind from somewhere underneath the blankets.

Grinning in the darkness, she placed the two objects on the mattress, next to his body. 'Anthony,' she whispered again, rocking him slightly. She removed the blankets from him and in the gloom, regarded his form. He was a pathetic figure. His skinny legs and pot belly made her want to laugh, and baulk in equal measures.

Still smiling, she slid his stained briefs down from his waist. There was an unpleasant, but familiar, waft as she struggled to get them over the flaccid bulge of his penis and balls. The stink made her eyes sting, just a little, but she'd smelled, even tasted, worse.

There was little resistance as she slipped the rotten underwear further down his legs, dropping them on the floor.

'Anthony,' she whispered again, her voice taking on a more salacious tilt.

A voice that always worked on TV.

He grunted.

At least he's compos mentis, she thought, laughing at using a phrase she remembered from school. She spat on her hand before caressing his balls. She took them in her hands and massaged them. Ironically, they had always been her favourite part of him. She had always enjoyed the feel of the two glands, and in the early days it had excited her that her touching them could illicit such a reaction from him. The way he would inhale, sharply each time she gripped them.

His flaccid penis began to twitch.

Exactly how she knew it would.

As it began to expand she slid her hand from his balls up to the expanding shaft of his cock. He'd never been what anyone might call big, but it had always been good enough for the job. In the past, of course. All in the past.

He began to shift as his cock stiffened. Her hand grasped it at the base and squeezed, applying just the right amount of pressure to ensure the blood flow required to give him a full erection could get through.

It didn't take long.

'Janice,' he murmured.

She almost laughed out loud.

'Yes, Anthony. It's Janice,' she whispered.

His hands grabbed her by the back of the head, and she stiffened, just for a moment. Memories of violent sex, of beatings, of his dick being forced down her throat deep enough to make her gag, and once or twice, even vomit. These images almost made her stop, but when she thought of where this vile thing had been, and the memory of inserting a tampon into her child's anus, it compelled her to continue.

Gordon's sobbing filled her ears while the blood mixed with shit was all she could smell.

This *was* going to happen. She was in charge now.

She pushed his hand away and continued massaging his cock.

She pulled the foreskin back from the tip, and the reek that assaulted her nostrils caused her to wince, to gag. It also, for some strange reason, caused her stomach to grumble. He'd never been one for personal hygiene, and whoever this Janice was, she obviously didn't mind either.

Fucking skank, she thought with a grin.

The foreskin was loaded.

It usually was.

The sharp stink of stale piss was what made her wince, along with the white build-up of smegma, which she knew would be residing there, was what made her stomach grumble. After all, cheese had been her favourite food since she was a child.

What made her really gag, what brought the tears of anger, was the underlying stink of shit.

It might have been the stink of her own shit. After all, he had forced this revolting flesh-stick into her ass—with only a little bit of spit as a lubricant—this very night.

She was also aware that it might not be her own ass she could smell on that tip. It could have been Janice's, whoever that was.

She wasn't even sure if the smell was real or not. It might have only been in her imagination. All she knew was that this think had been forced into places where no father's cock had any right to ever go. The vision of what he had done, and allowed to be done to her poor son's anus made her sick to her stomach.

But it also compelled her onwards with this mission.

She attempted to push all this nastiness from her head. She had a job to do, and they were doing nothing but make her procrastinate her duties.

She smiled at her use of the word procrastinate.

She was doing this *because* of those deeds, because of *Gordon*, and nothing now could stop her.

Closing her eyes, wishing herself somewhere else, she did the one thing she knew would wake him, and rouse him in a good mood.

She licked her teeth, produced some saliva, and opened her mouth.

Her spit was plentiful, as if her body, or her brain, knew what she was about to do and was attempting to combat the stink, the bacteria, and of course, the taste.

She knew this would be the very last time she would have his dick inside her—mouth, pussy, ass, it didn't matter. This would be the last time he penetrated her, or anyone, ever again. With this promise, she sealed her husband's fate.

She wrapped her lips around the putrid tip and sucked on it, just a little.

Anthony moaned.

Zola

It was working.

'Baby, is that you?' he whispered.

She didn't know if she was the *baby* he was referring to, but she didn't care. 'Uh huh,' she confirmed as she sucked again. She guessed it was the smegma that came away in her mouth, as she could feel *bits* on her tongue and on the back of her throat. She didn't care. She swallowed it; knowing that in the grand scheme of things, it didn't matter.

'Oh, fuck, yes …' he moaned again, reaching for the back of her head again.

She slipped him out of her mouth, ignoring the dribble of slime that drooled from his eye onto her lips, and looked up.

He was awake.

The stale stink of alcohol and farts had been replaced by the eye watering sharpness of his dick and the pre-cum leaking from his slit.

She laughed as the surprise on his face of seeing *her* head down there registered. He smiled too. When he did, he looked like the Anthony of old. The Anthony who she didn't mind doing what she was currently doing to. She had even enjoyed it.

But this wasn't *that* Anthony.

That Anthony was long gone, dead and buried. His stinking corpse was residing in the rotting sarcophagus she was currently blowing.

She grabbed his shaft tighter between her fingers and squeezed. He reacted exactly how she knew he would. He flexed, and his stomach tightened.

He was close. He never had been a stayer, unless he was too drunk to cum, that was usually when the beatings started.

She wanted him close, but not to cross the line. She stopped.

'Aw, baby … come on, I'm nearly there,' he breathed.

'I know,' she whispered. 'I want you to look at me when you cum.'

He grinned, shuffled up on the pillows and put his hands behind his head. 'Go on then,' he whispered.

She squeezed him again. He took another sharp breath. She massaged her hand up and down, up and down, up and down. 'Tell me when you're gonna cum,' she whispered, licking the tip of his cock. The smell not so bad now as her mouth, and her spit had cleaned away the majority of the filth.

His breathing became rapid. 'It's close … it's …'

She stopped what she was doing. 'Look at me,' she snapped.

His eyes snapped open. A stupid, almost vacant look spread across his face.

Fucking stupid cum face, she thought.

She reached down and picked up one of the items she'd placed on the bed. She held it up for him to see. Even though the room was gloomy, it wasn't full dark, she knew he could see it.

His ugly cum face disappeared in the wink of an eye.

The bread knife, the long one with the serrated edge, glinted, reflecting the poor light from the hallway. 'What …' he breathed.

'This is for Gordon, you cunt,' she hissed.

There was a dirty sock on the floor of the bedroom. She reached for it and stuffed it into his mouth. The shock of what she had just done was not lost on him and he drew in a deep breath, sucking the sock further into his mouth, silencing the scream that was on the tip of his tongue.

'*Do it,*' the devil version of herself perched on her shoulder whispered.

'*Cut his filthy fucking dick right off,*' the angelic version hissed.

In one hand, she gripped his erection, bringing the serrated edge of the knife down to his tip with the other. The thin, cold metal blade fit into his slit almost as if it was designed for this purpose.

As his body clenched, she smiled.

It was a sweet smile.

It was the same smile she used to flash him while wiping semen from her chin—or her hands, or her breasts—back in the days when their future looked rosy, when it felt like anything could, and just might, happen.

She pulled the hand holding the knife back.

The blade did the job it was supposed to do.

It cut!

It sliced!

It carved effortlessly through the swollen penis.

The blood was instant, plentiful, and surprisingly warm.

It spurted before it flowed. It sprayed over her face, into her open, expectant mouth, very much like the cum he'd been expecting, and that she had gotten so excited about in her youth.

The taste wasn't as bad as she thought it might be.

His mouth was comically wide, especially with the dirty sock hanging from it, but his eyes were wider. No sounds could escape the cotton gag. No sex moans, no swear words, no name calling… no screaming. He was almost as silent as the grave.

Pouting, she pushed her hand forward again, carving a deeper gash into the erection. The blade cut effortlessly, slicing his dick like the worst banana split ever conceived. She didn't slow to appreciate this dessert, however; she just continued to saw.

She marvelled at how easy it was, a lot easier than she thought it might have been.

Removing her slick, crimson hand from his shaft, she continued to cut. Both sides peeled away. It split right down the middle, slapping against his writhing, blood soaked thighs.

Anthony hadn't moved, except for his legs. They were twitching, thrashing, but they were no longer strong enough to hinder her work.

When she finished, she wiped her face with a blood-soaked hand, leaving a swathe of red across her mouth, giving her the comical appearance of a skewed clown, or even one of those transvestite drag queens she'd watched, and enjoyed on TV. His cack was split into two pieces of unidentifiable meat, languishing in a deep red gravy. He was thrashing around on the bed. The shock of what had just happened was hitting, and as the sock looked about to fall from his mouth, she knew the screaming was about to begin. Coolly, she reached for the second item she'd brought up with her from the kitchen.

A chunk of soft, ripe cheese.

She broke the chunk into two, and removing the sock from his quivering mouth, she stuffed it with one of the chunks, stifling his screams again. She then stuffed the other, blood smeared piece into his ruined crotch.

The agonising scream came, but it was stifled by cheese.

She leaned into the man she hadn't loved for years but, unfortunately, had tolerated. 'That's for Gordon, you pathetic little man,' she hissed, pushing the cheese deeper into the wound of his split cock.

His eyes rolled to the back of his head, and she could tell he was about to faint. She wanted him awake, as alert as he could be, for as long as she could get him, so she took the crumbs that had fallen from the cheese and rubbed them into his nostrils, before pushing the larger chunk in his mouth, deeper.

His arms flailed, his legs kicked, but she knew he would be in too much confusion, too much agony, to pose any threat to her mission.

His eyes calmed, and his brow creased. As he regarded his murderer, she smiled.

She took the cheese from his crotch. She regarded the yellow, blue-veined dairy, before licking the blood and gristle from it. She laughed, tipping her dying husband a wink before she ate it.

His eyes were screaming, silently, as they watched her tear one half of his penis from his body. It came away easily, too easily. She rubbed cheese onto that and ate it too.

'This is for what you and your sick fuck friends have been doing to my Gordon,' she whispered between loud chews.

His eyes were crazed, they were spinning in his sockets, they were somewhere else, watching his own personal Hell, but she knew he had an understanding of what was happening.

She was glad. She wanted him to know, to understand why he was in so much agony, why his wife had cut his cock in two, and ate it.

'I'm going to kill you now,' she whispered, wiping the blood and cheese from her chin. 'But before I do, I'm going to make you eat your own dick, you stinking, filthy prick.'

She had shocked herself with her use of bad language during this whole ordeal, but she figured if the angel on her shoulder could use it, then so could she. It rather fitted the moment anyway.

Anthony was moaning and writhing, attempting to escape the clutches of her mad-woman persona, but it was fruitless. There was nowhere he could go now. He *had* to die. She knew he wouldn't be able to live with only half a dick.

Using the slippery knife, she cut the remaining sliver of cock from his body. This was tougher than the first half, as the blood smeared handle kept sliding from her grasp. Finally, with the flopping morsel secure in her hands, she rubbed cheese into it and showed it to him. His eyes focused on the bloody hors d'oeuvre, the grim amuse bouche, before the cheese was pulled from his mouth and his own cock was stuffed in.

She pushed it as far as it would go.

He tried to resist, but he was far too weak.

She pushed the cheese infused penis down his gullet.

His eyes were so wide, they were in danger of popping out of his head. This made her smile, thinking about how wide her poor boy's eyes must have been when this animal, and his friends, were raping him.

This thought alone gave her the impetus she needed to give the cheesy fragment a final push.

He began to choke.

Good, she thought.

Zola

She removed her fingers from his mouth, not wanting to lose any digits in his thrashings. She then leaned back on the second set of blood-soaked sheets of the evening, to watch as the man she once loved, the man she had entrusted with her dreams, the man who taken that trust and smashed it into a million different pieces, choked to death on his own dick.

Well, half of it at least. She chuckled as her tongue played with a small morsel caught in one of her teeth.

He clawed at his throat. He raked at his skin. His bulging red eyes pleaded with her, cursed her, accused her.

She didn't care.

All she cared about was the cheese she'd used in this work. *What a waste,* she chuffed.

Anthony Zola died in his own bedsheets. There was cheese up his nose; in his ruined crotch that was nothing more than a mess of pumping blood and chinks of cheese, and half of his own dick, smeared with the very same cheese, was lodged down his throat.

Her work here was done.

5.

ANTHONY WAS DEAD.

Andrea now had another worry on her already overly stressed brain. What were they going to do now? She really hadn't thought this part through.

She scoffed at the idea of her having a plan. She'd been acting on pure impulse, no matter how cool and calm she'd been.

Now she was stuck with the conundrum of how to dispose of a body.

The effort of moving Anthony from the bed had exhausted her. She never would have thought that such a skinny little shit would have had so much dead weight. It took more than a few attempts, but she eventually managed to haul the bloated, purple body off the bed and into the wardrobe where his clothes still hung.

She closed the door and slid down it, wiping the strands of sweaty hair from her face. 'Done,' she told herself, although deep down, she knew it couldn't be his final resting place. The room was already starting to stink. Soon that reek would worm its way into all of her clothes. She suspected *she* would become nose blind, as would Gordon, but there would be others who would smell the decay.

They lived in a small, detached house in a rural, quiet part of town, so she wouldn't have to worry too much about neighbours, and neither she nor the boy had any real friends who might come calling, not without announcing anyway. Also, she had been home schooling Gordon for years.

So, she might just touch lucky.

~~~~

The boy was now fatherless.

That much was a blessing, but she worried about who might miss the bastard. She worried about his work colleagues reporting his absence, or the fact that he was suddenly missing from the bars he frequented.

However, as it turned out, she needn't have worried about any of it.

No one person missed him.

She had spent hours sitting next to the phone, her eyes closed, willing it not to ring. There hadn't been one call, not from work when he never turned up, not from the bars he drank in either. Apparently, he had been as popular there as he had been at home.

His family had kept their distance since their wedding. She had an inkling that his mother and father had died a few years back, but his brother and his sister had never tried to contact them, not even when Gordon was born.

I bet the only people who'll miss him are the dirty perverts he sold Gordon to, she thought, her face creasing into a rictus of hate as the vile thought passed.

The money from the box, and the extra she'd found after rifling through Anthony's clothing, would pay their rent for a while. As she held the piles of dollar bills in her hands, she thought about what they represented. Just how much must he have been sharing their son around for, to get such a return. With a quick estimation, she calculated there might be enough to live on for a couple of years, at least, paying the rent, the heating, and the electricity. The problem she could foresee was Gordon. He was a growing lad and would therefore need clothes and food.

She needed a plan to stretch the money.

Maybe I could get a job.

That was a non-starter for her. Apart from not having any marketable skills, she wouldn't be able to leave Gordon in the house, alone, for hours at a time, especially with his father's corpse stuffed in the wardrobe.

The must be another way.

She thought of entertaining men for money.

But she thought of how that would affect Gordon. The poor boy had been through enough, he didn't need to be privy to his mother turning tricks for money. There needed to be something else they could do to cut down on that would allow them to live. The rent just couldn't be missed. The last thing she needed was for the landlord, or God forbid the police, coming around and smelling the unmistakable stink of death that was already permeating around the house. The use of gas could be reduced during the summer, but it got cold during the winter, and they would need to keep warm.

Food and clothing were requirements too.

She nodded as she sat at the kitchen table, staring into the dirty window overlooking a small, overgrown garden.

Life was going to be tough from here on in.

~~~~

Flies had started to gather in the bedroom. The constant buzzing had gotten so bad, so annoying, she'd moved into Gordon's room to sleep with him. Also, no matter how hard she scrubbed, how much detergent, or soap she used, she could not rid the house of the stink of her rotting husband. When she'd gotten him into the wardrobe, she thought it might have been a while before he started to decay, and smell, and when it did start, it would only last for a few days.

However, the stench had started the very next day.

It was so bad; Gordon wouldn't come out of his room. He'd also been asking where his Daddy was.

She found herself totally unprepared for this level of questioning and didn't know how to answer them.

The boy was also complaining about being hungry.

She had routed through all the cupboards in the kitchen, to get an idea of how much food they had. All she could find were random tinned goods, cheese, and gin.

She regarded the cheese.

A memory hit her, it might have been a flashback, whatever it was, it rocked her to her heels. She was stuffing cheese into Anthony's groin. Next, she was eating the split dick with the cheese spread all over it.

Her stomach grumbled.

At first, she passed it off as nausea, from the disgusting memory, and she was just feeling sick. God knew she'd done enough throwing up in the few days since she did what she did.

Only this was different.

This was not nausea; this was hunger.

In her head she romanticised how it had tasted. Before she could be revulsed, she found her mouth filling with saliva. *How can that make me hungry?* she thought, then remembered she hadn't eaten anything in … *how long?* She didn't know. *Have I even fed Gordon?*

'Gordon, would you come down here please?' she shouted, not having the energy to make it to the stairs. 'Gordon …'

'Coming,' he replied.

She listened, smiling as his feet thumped along the landing. They stopped, she guessed it had been her room, *her old room,* before he continued downstairs.

As his head popped around the door, his smile broke her heart. There was so much love in it, so much innocence, even though all of it had been taken from him, ripped from him. The boy was such a delight, and it amazed her every single day that he'd managed to keep a modicum of that innocence, just for her.

'Are you hungry?' she asked.

He nodded.

She smiled and held her arms out to him.

He came to her and buried his head into her bosom.

Tears came again.

The moment passed, she wiped her eyes and made them some grilled cheese. She had to pick out the mould spots on the tough bread, but it was a decent meal, and they shared it together.

The smell of the grilled cheese overpowered the stink of the rancid Anthony, for a short while at least.

She was thankful for small mercies.

~~~~

Later, after Gordon was tucked up in bed, she found herself sitting at the kitchen table, the box of dollar bills open before her. She was staring out at the bare wall. Her face was almost as blank as the featureless structure before her. The grilled cheese sandwich she'd made Gordon's earlier was on her mind. More specifically, it was the smell of the sandwich that was still lingering, just underneath the sickly-sweet, thick stench of Anthony.

The fact the sandwich had masked the stink of death from skulking around the house had impressed her and given her an idea.

She went to the cupboard and opened a block of cheese. It was a particularly smelly blue. One of her favourites. She sniffed it, and her stomach rumbled.

Some people might consider the smell putrid, but she found it beautiful, and she wanted it.

The idea that had been bouncing around her head, attempting to free itself, was then fully realised.

Taking the package, she left the kitchen and made her way upstairs.

She lingered outside her bedroom, her hand hovering over the handle. She could hear Gordon's thin, nasally breathing. She smiled as she gripped the handle, and let herself in.

A black cloud attacked her instantly. The buzz of the fat bluebottles filled the air. There must have been hundreds, if not thousands of the beasts, hovering, buzzing, dive-bombing. The stink was thick, almost physical. Her stomach flipped, and her mouth was instantly filled with saliva. She could taste the vomit and knew it was close, perhaps too close. She bowed her head, opened her mouth, and prepared herself for the projectile extraction.

It never came.

Instead, she caught a whiff of the cheese in her hand, and the stink of her dead husband went away. The flies were still there, but she thought she could deal with them. Her stomach began to settle a little. The cocktail of smells coming from the cheese and Anthony's ripe body, kind of complimented each other.

Suddenly her mouth was watering again, albeit for a different reason.

She was hungry again.

Slowly, she made her way to the wardrobe. She paused, waving away the flies that were amassing around her cheese, and around the door. Gritting her teeth, she unclipped the latch, and the door fell open.

Another, blacker cloud escaped the tight space, surrounding her. Panic swelled, as for just a moment she found herself lost in an all-encompassing fuzz. In her confusion, she wondered what it could have been. Could it have been the black, ghostly hand of Anthony coming back to wreak horrible revenge on her for what she'd done to him? Only when the horrible tickle of insect legs crawling on her face, as they attempting to enter her nose, and grouping in the corners of her eyes, did she realise it was flies.

The haze was fat from feasting on rotting flesh.

As the bloated insects crawled into her mouth, she accidently crunched one or two of them. The taste of Anthony's decay sliding down her throat hit her like a slap in the face. Her stomach began to do its thing again. She raised the cheese to her nose, took another deep sniff, and it settled, just like that. She looked at the bloated, purple-skinned body stuffed inside the small wardrobe, and blew some foul smelling air from between her lips. There was a thick pool of congealed blood at the bottom, and his crotch looked like a wild animal had been at it. Little white worms were wriggling in the wound; it took her moment to realise they were maggots, thousands of the things. She honestly thought, if it wasn't for the delicious smell of cheese, she would be vomiting uncontrollably now.

The wound had congealed, yet it was still wet.

She didn't care.

The smell was hideous.

She didn't care about that either.

Spitting more of the huge dirty flies from her mouth, she leaned in, holding the pack of cheese, and rubbed it on his purple, bruised flesh.

It was cold, and it was wet. A layer of skin peeled away, onto the cheese as she rubbed it in. It repulsed her in the first instance, but once the stink of the dairy conjoined with the sickly-sweet decay, it didn't seem anywhere near as bad as it had been. *Maybe I'm getting used to it*, she thought. It was either that or it could have been something else entirely. All she knew was that Anthony was now smelling almost …

Don't even think that, she scolded herself.

But he is … the other side of her brain argued.

He's not, and never will be …

He is, though!

She let herself drop to the floor. A colony of flies that had been resting there, bathing in her husband's congealed mess, raised up, angry at being disturbed as they feasted, fucked, and laid their eggs in the new eutopia they'd found.

It would certainly solve a problem, she reasoned. *Maybe two…*

Would it, though? Or would it just raise a whole host of new ones?

She shuffled on her backside, moving away from the cadaver and the, now wonderful, aroma of its decay mixed with the noble smell of veined cheese.

Her stomach was shouting at her. It couldn't believe how suddenly delicious the smell was.

She needed to get out of this room. Strange thoughts were spiralling through her head, thoughts that had no right to be there.

But they made sense.

Zola

It could get us through a tough patch. Just until Gordon is old enough to stay home on his own so I can get a job and bring in enough money for us to live on and to ...

She paused the rambling in her head. It all made perfect sense to her. *It would kill two birds with one stone.* She kicked the wardrobe doors closed and left the room.

She needed time to think.

6.

SHE DIDN'T SLEEP that night.

They had eaten and eaten well. She had taken them out to the diner that was less than a mile from where they lived. They had walked, as Andrea had never learned to drive. She decided that spending a little of the money on a slap-up meal would give her head space to ponder on their predicament, plus it would be a nice little outing for Gordon.

He had wanted pizza with extra cheese, she had selected a chicken and cheese omelette.

Both dishes were chosen without irony, a thought she realised a little later while walking home.

'Mummy, where's Dad?' Gordon asked as he tucked into his ten-inch pizza.

Andrea smiled. Inside she was running on empty, but she just had to keep it together for her boy. She wanted him to have the most normal upbringing she could give him, but she didn't want to lie to him. 'He's gone, sweetheart,' she said as the last forkful of omelette was scooped off her plate. She looked at the chunk of chicken skewered on the tines of her fork. Its yellow skin with grease oozing from it, and the cheesy goodness coating it, made her mouth water. She had another flashback; it was Anthony's penis, sawn in half and dripping with blood, and cheese.

When her mouth filled with saliva, it wasn't for the cheap omelette. It was for something else.

'Gone where?' Gordon continued.

Her eyes closed as she popped the morsel into her mouth and began to chew it, savouring the grease. 'Just gone, sweetie.'

'Will he be coming back?'

She laughed. 'I hope not,' she whispered.

Gordon seemed to have gotten the joke, as he laughed too. 'Good. I never really liked him anyway. Him, or his friends.'

With the smile still on his lips, he continued to tuck into his pizza.

She nodded.

Her mind was made up.

~~~~

As they made to leave the diner, a strange thing happened. She was at the counter, paying, when Gordon's demeanour changed. Suddenly shy, he pushed himself behind her, obviously trying to hide from something.

'What's up, sweetie?' she asked.

He didn't answer, he just gripped the back of her coat and buried his head into her back.

'Hey, little man,' the man behind the till greeted Gordon. 'Long time, no see.' He offered the boy a wink.

Gordon continued to cower behind Andrea, his chubby hands tugging at her coat.

'You're Tony's kid, aren't you?' the man continued, not caring a bit that he was scaring the boy.

'Excuse me, could you not talk to my boy, please?' Andrea snapped.

The man looked at her, and a grin spread across his face as his eyes roamed over her, up and down. The violation disagreed with her, and a shiver travelled down her spine. He was nodding now. 'Yeah, you're Tony's wife. He showed us the pictures …'

He let the sentence trail off, and Andrea blushed. She thought the heat in her face might melt her flesh. She remembered the pictures Anthony had her pose for. He told her they were only for him, something to look at when he was alone at work, or if she were out enjoying herself.

They had been explicit. Very explicit.

'Come on, Gordon. We're leaving,' she snapped, throwing the money for the meal on the desk next to the till.

'Gordon? Yeah, you *are* Tony's little boy.' The man grinned. 'Where've you been, little man? We've been missing you at the club, you and your old man. You know, you were very popular.'

Andrea glared at him. She grabbed Gordon and pulled him away, out of the diner.

'We miss you, little man,' he shouted as they left.

Andrea could still hear him laughing as she tried to sleep that night.

7.

THERE WAS AN electric knife in one of the drawers. It was still in the box, an unwanted, unneeded wedding present from someone she had never seen again after that day. She unwrapped it and applied both blades. She looked at them and grinned. They looked like the blades from the bread knife. They brought back some bittersweet memories.

She looked around the kitchen, making sure Gordon hadn't seen her guilt. He hadn't, he wasn't in the room, he was upstairs watching TV in his room. She was glad about that.

Tonight, she had promised him something special for supper, and she was not about to let him down, the boy had endured his fair share of disappointment in this life.

Wrapping a tea-towel around her face, she entered the fly infested room and turned on the lights. The bare bulb hardly cast any illumination, such was the plague of flies swarming around the lightbulb and the windows. The room was bleak. *Fitting for what I'm about to do,* she thought, avoiding opening her mouth in case any of the flies flew in, even beneath the towel.

Swallowing, just trying to lubricate her dry throat, she opened the door to the wardrobe. His remains were still there, in a crumpled, rotting pile. With this level of decay came an even worse smell. She'd taken the precaution of rubbing cheese beneath her nose prior to entering the room.

It had helped.

Actually, it *enhanced* the experience.

She likened it to entering a favourite restaurant. The smells that were mingling were intoxicating. She smacked her lips together, surprising herself in the anticipation of what she was about to do. She grabbed one of her ex-husband's wasting arms. She overjudged her grip, and her fingers squelched as the rotten, miscoloured skin split beneath her fingers. They passed through the cold, clammy flesh, almost to the bone.

The open wound released more stink, and the aroma became quite exquisite. She wanted to taste it, to sample it, to savour it.

Her stomach grumbled.

She looked at the damp mess on her hands.

Even through the towel, she could smell the putrid delicacy. She envisioned the rancid deposit on her hand mixing with pale, veiny cheese, enriching the delicious, natural bacteria.

Her stomach grumbled again.

She looked behind her, through the mess of flies, to make sure the bedroom door was still closed.

It was.

Licking her lips again, marvelling in the fact that her mouth had gone from dry, to lubricated in a matter of moments, she crumbled a small amount of cheese and clenched her fist. She squeezed. The warm cheese mixed with the filth in the palm of her hand. It merged, it became something else, something almost liquid … and fantastic.

Closing her eyes, she envisioned a posh French restaurant. On the fancy plate before her was a delightful melee of rotten, jelly-like human flesh, mould, and fermented diary products.

Her stomach was in turmoil now.

It craved the delicacy. It wanted her to fill her lungs with the exotic bouquet, to tease her tastebuds with it. It longed for her to swill the mess around her mouth, before swallowing it, savour the taste, and the aftertaste.

Without thinking, she lifted the towel, and stuffed her wet fingers in her moist mouth, flies and all.

As she relished the unexpected crunch of the insects, a shiver ran through her.

Her body was instantly covered in goosebumps.

Her head began to swim.

Everything in the world was suddenly… different.

All the bad things, everything that had happened over the weeks, months, even years dissolved. Her situation changed, enhanced. She and her boy were saved. Everything was going to be OK from here on in.

She had found something. Something good. *Better than good, she thought.* It was something that could sustain her and Gordon's situation for a long time to come.

'Tony and cheese,' she giggled, no longer minding the flies crawling into her mouth. She crunched a few more, enjoying the thick juice sliding down her throat as they popped.

'Croutons,' she giggled again, as a giddiness enveloped her.

Wasting no more time, and with renewed faith in life, she set onto the decrepit corpse with the electric carving knives.

Before long, she had multiple strips of meat laid out on the floor. The flies were swarming over them, but she didn't mind. In between the mounds of meat were puddles of wet fat. Rubbing the cheese in her hands, she mixed it with the fat before smearing it over the steaks.

Smiling, she regarded Anthony's decimated cadaver. There wasn't much left of him, she had stripped him almost to the bone. She had opened his stomach, allowing the half-digested, rotten food, that would have ruined the meat, to spill to the floor in a slurry. She scooped this offal into a bin bag. She would take it to the local park after dark tonight, where the stray dogs, cats, foxes, racoons, and anything else that might want a slice of her generosity, could fight for it until there was nothing left.

She looked at the fully prepared cheese steaks. There were quite a few of them, more than enough for them to eat tonight, and maybe even for the next few days. She decided to freeze the rest for future consumption. She didn't know how long human flesh stayed fresh, but she guessed it would be pretty much the same as chicken or pork.

Fresh, she laughed. *He's been here for ages. If he was going off, it would have been ages ago.*

She stood, brushing clumps of her husband, and cheese from her lap.

Zola

With a nod, she left the room, carrying her bounty in the Tupperware containers she'd brought with her. She slipped some of the steaks into freezer bags, lying two at time in each bag. When she was done, she estimated there was maybe three months worth of dining ahead of them.

She also had an idea where she could find more of the same, for when Anthony was all used up.

~~~~

'Will Daddy be coming back?' Gordon asked as he tucked into his steak that was slathered in cheese.

Andrea smiled. 'Not unless you're sick tonight, baby. Now come on, don't let him ruin a good meal. Are you enjoying it?'

The boy made a slurping noise and licked his lips. 'Delicious,' he said, shoving another bite into his mouth.

Andrea smiled, taking another chunk of her own steak into her mouth.

~~~~

That night, while Gordon slept, Andrea took a lump hammer from the tool shed and ground up Anthony's body, bones, and all.

She carried the remains to the kitchen, where she mixed the bits with rosemary, thyme, some garlic, salt and pepper to season it, and a lot of cheese. She then boiled up the mix.

61

For the next few weeks, Andrea and Gordon ate like royalty on cheese steaks and her very own special broth.

'If you eat all your food, you'll grow up big and strong,' she fussed. 'Just like Daddy.'

She laughed then, as if this was the best joke in the whole world.

Zola

8.

EVERYTHING WENT WELL for a few months. Until one evening, Andrea noticed their Anthony supplies were dwindling.

There was an hour, maybe more, where panic's icy fingers twisted in her gut, putting questions like, *what are you going to do*? in her head. She could go out and spend a little of the remaining money, which was also dwindling, on groceries, or she could carry out the plan she had devised many moons ago, when Anthony's cheese steaks were still plentiful.

She entered the bedroom. The flies and the stink of death were mostly gone now, although she suspected there might be a residual smell lingering in the room, she couldn't tell as she was used it.

With a deep sigh, she removed one of her few decent dresses, the ones she had bought with the money from *that bastard,* before she knew where it was coming from. She looked the garment over, searching for gore or dried blood encrusted into it, like with most of her other clothing. Relieved not to find anything, she hung it on the window, sprayed it with air freshener, and tried it on.

It still fit.

Maybe human meat is good for you, she laughed. *The Anthony diet!*

She looked at herself in the mirror, straightening the dress over her ample curves, and nodded. 'This will do,' she whispered.

Sitting at her dressing table, she applied some makeup. She hadn't done this in a long while and was way out of practice.

Making sure Gordon was asleep, she crept downstairs and exited the house. She loitered for a small while on the other side of the door, pondering what she was about to do. She knew it was the right thing, for her and for her boy, but it *felt* wrong somehow.

Vengeance is a dish best served cold, she thought. *But I prefer mine with cheese.*

~~~~

The bar was dark, smoky, and full. It was a mostly male patronage, but there were a few women dotted around. They were swamped by lecherous men, all of them vying for their attention. She knew this was one of the places Anthony frequented, and she knew it was a place he frequented with his *so-called* friends.

She just needed to find them.

It didn't take long until they found her.

The same man from the till at the diner approached her as she sat alone at the bar. 'I know you, don't I?' he slurred, setting himself into the vacant stool next to her.

She smiled. It was a coy smile. One filled with innocence, naivety, and hidden purpose. She squinted as she looked at him. 'I think so,' she whispered. 'You were friends with my husband. We, that's me and my son, Gordon, were at the diner a while back. You recognised him. You knew Anthony.'

At the use of her son's and her husband's names, the man began to back off. 'Hey, I'm not messing with any married women,' he hissed. 'I got enough problems with one of them at home.'

'Oh, I'm not married anymore,' she gushed, taking a handkerchief from her purse and dabbing her eyes with it.

'Single?' he asked, cocking his head. 'Tony's gone? I'm so sorry to hear that,' he said, sitting back down. He took one of her hands and squeezed it. 'We wondered why he hadn't been around. What happened?'

She swallowed and sniffed, while nodding.

'He just split on me.' She smiled inwardly as she thought about how this was, quite literally, the truth. She dabbed her eyes again. 'I think the rotten bastard just choked on us.'

'Tony Zola, huh?' he replied, shaking his head, and taking a sip of his drink.

'How's the boy, what was his name again?'

'Gordon,' she replied a little too quickly, and she cursed inwardly.

'Gordon, that's it. Cute little guy,' he said with a laugh.

Fuck you, you perverted, child raping cunt, she thought, smiling, and dabbing her eyes again. 'He's a little cutie all right.'

'Me and all the fellas were wondering why he stopped coming around. We miss that little guy.'

I bet you do!

'It was so sudden,' she gushed. 'He just cut his losses and went.' *I'm pretty good at this,* she laughed in her head.

The man took her hand and gripped it tight. 'That must be awful.'

She smiled her best sad smile. 'It has been. I've been so lonely, stuck in the house, all on my own. I just needed to get out. I needed a little …' she looked up at him, her eyes blazing. The man grinned, it was a horrible, knowing smile. '…adult company. If you know what I mean.'

He nodded. 'I know exactly what you mean, and that's just what you've got with me,' he whispered.

~~~~

Two hours later, they were back at her house. They were both naked, and she had another penis in her mouth.

Beneath the mattress they were sharing, hidden but easily to hand, was a large bread knife, a sock, and a big old chunk of cheese.

Part Two:

Gordon

1.

AS THE YEARS passed, Gordon grew to be a well-balanced, handsome, and well-adjusted young man. During his teenage years, he made the conscious decision to forgo hanging out in the malls and chasing girls on his bike with his friends. He decided not to join the softball team in school, or the football team even though the coach almost begged him to. He never went to the prom either, he decided he wanted to be a good son and stay home to keep his mother from getting lonely.

This was in Andrea's head, of course.

Gordon grew to become an unbalanced, overweight, maladjusted man-child. Due to his inactivity, he piled on an inordinate amount of weight. He had never had his hair cut, he never shaved, and very seldom bathed.

He didn't do any school activities, mostly because he never went to school, and never had any friends to do them with anyway. The boy had fallen through the cracks of society and was not missed. Andrea had attempted to home school him. She wanted to keep him away from the ravages of a social life, and from corruptive external influences that might turn a boy's head, especially one with such a gentle a soul as he had.

She fed him, clothed him, and catered for his every whim.

It had only ever been the two of them.

Just them.

No one else.

They were as close as peas in pods, as tight as new shoes, as she liked to say. In the twelve years since his father had deserted them, he hadn't ever, not even once, left her side.

There had been other men in their lives. Many of them in fact. More than he could remember. When, and if, he ever met them, they were introduced to him as her *gentlemen callers*. Most stayed only for a few hours, maybe once or twice a week, and were never seen or heard from again. There were a few constants about these callers; once they had visited, he would always get new clothes, his mother usually had a little extra money, and his favourite meals would be on the menu for at least the next few weeks.

This was his mother's very own recipe for cheese steak and best of all, her special broth. The steaks were filleted meat, which he thought must have been chicken or pork, it was white meat at any rate, and they always came with the most delicious cheese sauce smeared and baked over them.

The thought of his mother spending time with these men always made his mouth water because he knew it meant there would be plenty of tasty dinners coming his way.

Sometimes, Andrea would go a little overboard with his food. This mostly occurred right after one of her *gentleman callers* had been. When this happened, he would usually end up eating a little too much. It was a good thing that the clothes his mother gave him after a *gentleman caller* had gone were mostly a larger size than he needed.

Life was good. He'd never known anything different.

He was content and he was happy. They had each other, and only needed others in their lives every now and then.

No one had come calling to find out where his father had gone, and after a while, Anthony began to fade from Gordon's memory. Occasionally, there would be dreams. Dreams where men in cloaks with dark faces stood around him in a circle in rooms filled with candles. In these dreams, he would be passed around. They would touch him, he thought it might have been inappropriately, but then he'd never had much of a grasp of what was inappropriate or not.

Over the years, he grew.

His inactivity and his social isolation grew too.

In his mother's eyes, and in his, there was nothing wrong with this. However, others, outsiders, the men who came calling and he never saw leave, he always felt they looked at him as if he was a freak.

His mother usually told him to hide when the men called. He would cower in his room, usually with an extra cheese steak or a big bowl of broth to keep him occupied. Occasionally he would creep up to her room and peek. Sometimes he would see the men treating his mother badly. Usually this made him angry, and he would run and cry in his room.

'It fucking stinks in here,' some of them would complain.

'Don't you ever clean this place?' others would say.

He watched as some of them kissed her, not mindful of the stink. He hated that. It always built up his hopes that he might get a new father. Someone new in their lives. A man he could look up to. However, he never saw any of these men again. All he got, in place of the desired paternal presence, was more cheese steak and second-hand clothing.

A few times, the men caught him watching them.

They would recoil, shouting that something weird was spying on them from the door. 'What the fuck is that?' he would hear them ask.

His mother would soothe them, telling them it was nothing. That *he* was nothing.

This hurt his feelings. If his mother thought he was nothing, *then, am I nothing?* he would ask himself.

These situations were always followed by moaning, some banging, a scream or two, then periods of prolonged silence. After the silence came noises, like an electric knife cutting through something.

When the noises stopped, mother would wash.

That was when he would peep again.

He enjoyed watching her lather up her fleshy, pink body. Especially the mounds she had on her chest. They looked like the mounds he had on his chest, but hers were less hairy, and they hung lower. He loved seeing her big red nipples and the hairy part between her legs covered in soap. Watching always gave him a funny feeling in his stomach, and it would make his *thingus*, that was what his mother called it, get bigger and harder. He enjoyed that feeling the most. One of the nicest parts of watching his mother wash was the colour of the water in the tub. It would usually be pink, and he wondered how she got it like that. On the odd occasion when he bathed, the water would just be grey, not the exotic pink like hers.

This disappointed him.

When mother was washed and the funny feeling in his *thingus* was gone—usually after his knees had buckled, his white stuff had sprayed out, and the itchy wetness had begun—then it was his favourite time.

Dinner time.

Suddenly, the freezer would be stocked. It would be crammed full of his favourite cheese steaks, and there would always be a huge pot of broth bubbling away on the stove.

This was always followed by long periods of just the two of them. There would be no *gentlemen callers,* and they would stay inside together, playing cards and telling stories.

He loved this time.

It was his most favourite.

2.

MORE YEARS PASSED this way, and Gordon kept on getting bigger. He was now a grown man. In reality, he was more than that, he was almost as big as two grown men. Obese was not a word he knew, he only knew the ones his mother had taught him, but that was what he was. He was flabby, scabby, pasty, and pale. He was also very hairy.

His hair hung down his back in knotted, greasy rattails. His face was covered in a thick, filthy beard. There were clumps of food, skin, and other things hiding in there, some were alive, others were not. He enjoyed the alive ones tickling him as they crawled, ate, burrowed, fucked, and laid their eggs. There were entire generations of creatures living on him. His huge body was pale in places, red in others, and white and flaking everywhere else. Devoid of the sun, and mostly devoid of soap, he would rake at his skin, eating what he found beneath his fingernails, no matter what part of his body he scratched.

He had aged, as had his mother.

Zola

The *gentlemen callers* were now few and far between. They *would* come, however. They would gag and retch as they entered the house, but she was always there with a thick iron bar she kept behind the door. She would whack them over the head, and he watched them fall. He enjoyed seeing the thick red liquid, and the other stuff, ooze from their heads. His favourite part was when it splattered over the walls.

As she got older, she needed his help to get the men into the kitchen. 'I'm not as young as I used to be,' she'd complain, rubbing the small of her flabby back. 'Would you rub my back for me?' she'd ask.

He was always more than happy to do this.

He loved the feel of his mother's back. The warm, moist layers of flesh felt incredible beneath his grubby fingers. He would push them deep into the flab, getting excited by the way the soft pink skin absorbed them, sucking them in. The smell of her always made him hungry and doing this never failed to make his *thingus* grow. When he was done, when she was asleep, he would hide in his bedroom and rub something of his own, something that wasn't anywhere near as flabby as his mother's back. He would sniff his hands as he did this, enjoying the smell of his mother mixed with the stinging, cheesy stink of his stiff *thingus*. He would rub it until his feet began to tingle. He loved that feeling as he knew when it came, it would make his head feel fuzzy, just before the white stuff would come.

He loved it when the white stuff came most of all.

Once, he'd caught it in his hands and rushed to show his mother, but she'd told him to go and wash his hands and never show her anything like that again. This had saddened him, but it didn't stop him from doing it.

Whatever white stuff he could catch, he would keep in a jar, hidden under his bed where she couldn't find it. Sometimes, when he was hungry in the middle of the night, he would dip his fingers into the jar and sniff the strange aroma. He craved that weird smell. It reminded him of when his mother would clean the kitchen after a *gentleman caller* had visited. He knew it was wrong, and she would never approve, especially after chastising him about showing it to her, but he would put his fingers into his mouth and lick the sticky liquid off them, slipping his tongue into the grimy areas between his fingers, and raking his teeth underneath his black fingernails, making sure none of the gorgeous white stuff was missed.

It was cold and a little salty. But most of all, it was good.

He always put the jar back, happy in the knowledge that what he had just eaten, he would be able to refill again tomorrow.

As he got older, his mother got larger, meaning there were fewer *gentlemen callers*. When they did come, the cheese steaks got tougher. He didn't mind this too much. He didn't want much out of life. Just food, his mother, and the fun of rubbing his *thingus* while thinking about her.

Occasionally he remembered how sweet and tender the steaks had been in his youth. But he was content; as his mother kept telling him, life was good. Sometimes it was itchy, it was usually smelly, but it was good.

Then, everything changed, and life would never be the same again.

Zola

3.

HE AWOKE IN his bed—or what passed for a bed, basically it was a frame, topped by a worn-out mattress mostly held together by threads, dried cum, hard food, and old clothes stuffed inside, but it was comfortable. As his eyes adjusted to the gloom of the thin light streaming through the threadbare curtain, he stretched. Cobs of crust peeled away from his arms and legs, nestling in the folds of the rag he used as a blanket.

He eyed them, hungrily.

Something felt different about this morning. He couldn't quite put his finger on what it was, but there was a nagging feeling in the pit of his stomach that warned him that today would be special.

He wasn't quite sure if that would be special-good, or special-bad.

Normally, he would hear his mother fussing around, either downstairs or in one of the other rooms, but this morning, the house was silent. Sometimes she would go out—to do errands, as she called it—and maybe come back with a *gentleman caller*, so he was not overly worried about the silence. But he couldn't shake the *something* that was niggling

75

him. He sat up, his pink folds straining again with the effort. He stretched again, and this time, a veritable avalanche of clumps of dead skin tumbled from the various scabs that covered his body, inside his armpits, underneath his man boobs, from his hair and, of course, his beard.

A bloated insect scurried out of his crotch. He always enjoyed that tickle. He caught it, grinning at his fast reflexes. *Fastest hand in the West,* he thought. He held the beast in his fingers, attempting to identify what it could be, marvelling at its size, wondering where it could have been hiding, and if the thing had a family. He shrugged before popping the wriggling monster into his mouth, enjoying the crunch as his teeth ground it down.

Then came the pop.

He scratched at his crotch, addressing the annoying itch down there and hoping to maybe find another tasty treat. He loved this part of the morning. He liked that his *thingus* was usually hard, even thought it was sometimes difficult for him to tell, as it was usually tucked away within layers of flab. He stroked it a few times, thinking about his mother's globes in the bath. He touched his own globes, ignoring the course hair that covered them. He could feel the tingling beginning in his feet before travelling up his legs and along the length of his *thingus,* making its way to the tip.

Then he groaned.

The white stuff shot from it, landing on his stomach and bed sheets, adding to the build-up already between the layers of both. It also dripped, wet and warm, over his hand.

He scooped some out of his deep bellybutton and sniffed it.

There was more than a hint of his favourite dish in the smell, cheese steak, but with an undercurrent he thought of as exotic. He looked around the room, hoping his mother was not around, watching him, because he knew what he was about to do was ... *what was the word she used again? Inappropriate?*

He confirmed he was alone. There was no one stopping him from what he was about to do.

The pearlescent substance in his hand was making his mouth water. He grinned. It was a sly one that said, *I'm about to do something I shouldn't,* before licking his fingers. He'd tasted this before, usually cold from his jar, but it was so much better when it was fresh and warm.

'It's a taste sensation,' he laughed in his thick voice.

His mouth exploded with saliva as he swashed the oyster around his mouth, his tongue savouring the strange tastes. There was his favourite, cheese, or course. This was complimented by a grittiness that was never in the steaks his mother made. There was salt, and something else, a taste he could never identify. All he could think was it tasted ... white. There was no other way of describing it any better than that; just *white.* The only other time he tasted it was when he indulged in, what he liked to call, his Gordon Cakes.

It was a strange taste, but he did enjoy it.

He had another rummage between his thighs and came out with handful, that was caked in with flaked skin, coarse black hair, and a little something from the crack of his behind. He grinned. 'Bonus,' he mumbled before packing this mix into a Gordon Cake shape and eating it. He made special efforts to make sure that between his fingers, and his fingernails, were clean of the cake. He didn't want any to go to waste.

He could still smell it. He rubbed his hand through his beard, catching some of the wet mess in his fingers. It was now lukewarm. *It goes cold so quick*, he thought with a hint of sadness before putting four of his fingers into his mouth.

He removed the hairs from his tongue, scraping them onto the already sodden bedsheets before getting up to start his day.

The odd feeling he had awoken to returned.

'Mum,' he shouted, opening his bedroom door. He no longer bothered dressing, as the clothes his mother brought him these days were mostly too tight around his bulk. She had attempted to sew some of them together to make them fit, but now, if it was warm enough, he just preferred to walk around naked.

He liked the idea of his mother watching him as he did.

No one answered his call.

'Mother,' he shouted again, only for his calls to fall into empty rooms.

The house was indeed deserted.

It was as silent as the grave.

That was one of his mother's favourite sayings. He chuffed at the thought as he made his way downstairs to warm up a bowl of broth. There was still a bit left from the last *gentleman caller*.

As he traversed the steps, he just couldn't shrug off the nasty feeling hanging over him. It felt like a dark cloud on an otherwise sunny day. The kitchen was empty. The pot was on the stove, where it usually was, with a

78

smaller pan next to it. He spooned some of the clumpy, greasy soup into the smaller pan and lit the gas beneath it. He then turned his back on the broth and took in his surroundings.

The smell from his breakfast wafted up his nose.

He sucked it in deep, savouring the aroma.

Life is good, he thought as he turned off the gas and wiped the spoon in the pot into his wet armpit, hoping to remove some of the crustier particles that were stuck to it. Satisfied, he plunged the utensil into the broth. Another thing he'd noticed, as mother had gotten older, was the chunks in the broth had become bigger. It was almost as if she couldn't break the croutons down as much as she used to. He didn't mind, though; there was always something to chew, or crunch, and it would *always* be his most favourite part.

Sucking on the spoon, he wondered what he could to do with himself today. He hoped Mother would bring another *gentleman caller* back, as he could do with a little excitement. It would give him something to watch.

He hated when the house was so quiet.

It gave him chills.

Since the TV had broken a few years ago, he mostly had to find his own amusement.

Taking the pan with him, he decided to mooch around the house, as there was always the possibility she was doing something quiet in another room. She liked to read, and when she did, there was always the chance of her falling asleep. *Maybe that's what she's doing now,* he thought, trying to make himself feel less afraid. He'd never thought of being alone before, but right now, it was scaring him.

'Mum,' he shouted, looking up the stairs. 'Mummy?'

There was no answer.

The black cloud hanging over his head grew thicker and began to descend, just a little. It was heavy and threatening to envelop him, to wrap him in its evil darkness. It wanted to make him its slave.

'Mummy,' he shouted again, doing his best to keep the hysteria he could feel building within him, from his voice. The creaking of the wood under his feet was louder than usual, and his skin tightened as goosebumps crawled all over his naked body. Suddenly, the house was freezing. It was so cold that it bit into his voluminous flesh. All the nice feelings between his legs were gone, replaced with a horrible crawling a million times worse than the tickling of the insects living within his crevices.

He thought he could see the silence creeping down the stairs, like a mist slithering towards him, threatening to fuse with the ugly cloud over his head.

If they merged, he *knew* they would suffocate him.

'Mother!' he screamed in a high pitched shrill.

There was still no answer.

He put the pan on the floor, where instantly it was attacked by the flies that were a constant congregation in the house. Flies he could live with, he had done all his life, silence from his mother on the other hand, he couldn't.

Braving another stair, he stepped closer to her room, towards whatever the bad vibe he was feeling was so desperate to reveal to him. He shook his head, and another avalanche of bits fell from him. 'Stop it, Gordon,' he scolded. 'She's just out, finding another *gentleman caller*, that's all.' He wanted to believe this, he really did, but something was telling him otherwise.

A voice, one he thought might only be in his head, was shouting at him, warning him not to go into her room.

Very soon, he'd wish he'd listened.

He opened the door, slowly.

It was dark inside, glum, but then there was nothing strange about that. It kind of comforted him. He hadn't known what to expect, but to see it as it should be, how it had always been, was a comfort. His eyes soon adjusted to the twilight, and he sighed as he saw the silhouette of his mother, she was still in bed. The blankets were bunched over her ample hips, and her hair was spread over the pillow.

She was facing away from him, towards the window.

He smiled.

Good. He breathed.

Then, a naughty thought crawled into his head.

Is she naked too?

As this thought emerged, a delicious feeling, a sensual tingle, stirred below his waist. Silently, he stepped into the room, careful not to let the door slam behind him, or to step on the floorboards he knew creaked. It wasn't the first time he'd snuck into her room. As he made his way towards the bed, one hand found its way into the folds beneath his stomach, where he could feel his *thingus*. He gripped it, anticipating a little more Gordon Cake once he'd done what he came in here to do.

He reached the bed and peered over the mound of covers.

Result, he thought.

She *was* naked.

A shiver ran through him as he licked his lips. His eyes darted around the room, hoping not to find anyone there, watching him, accusing him. He was alone except for his sleeping mother. He was always alone, but it didn't stop him from worrying. Swallowing, marvelling at how dry his mouth had become in just a few moments, he began to play with himself. It was his all time, favourite this to do. He wished he could do it all the time. As his eyes crawled over her flabby breasts and the large purple nipples, he drooled. The familiar rush surged through his chest making his heart beat faster. Maybe a little too fast. The inevitable was happening, but it was happening too soon. He hadn't anticipated it coming this fast, but before he knew it, he'd passed the point of no return, the vinegar strokes—as he liked to call it, because he usually got a strong whiff of vinegar coming from the little slit in its head—far too soon.

His knees buckled, he closed his eyes and opened his mouth, allowing the moan that was battling within him to escape. He arched his back … then he came.

The white stuff spurted from his *thingus*.

He was too late to try to catch it, and it flew forth, landing over his mother's face and her breasts.

He felt like his heart missed a beat then, he felt dizzy and sick, all at the same time. He didn't want her to know he did this kind of thing, and he didn't want her to experience his white stuff, not all over her beautiful face.

His feet were lead. He couldn't have moved them, no matter how hard he tried. He had absolutely no idea what to do next. He kind of had the idea that the *gentlemen callers* did this kind of thing to her, and he knew what happened to them afterwards.

He didn't want his mother to make cheese steaks out of him.

He stood at the side of her bed with his back to the window, his wilting, dripping *thingus was* still in his hand. He was looking at the woman he loved the most in the whole world, petrified at how he would explain to her what had just happened.

It was then he realised that she hadn't moved. Not even a twitch, or a flinch when his white stuff spattered over her.

He thought he'd gotten away with it, this time at least.

He began to creep away from the bed, tucking his dripping *thingus* back between his fleshy thighs, when something else dawned on him. He'd left his white stuff all over her face. She'd wake up and smell it, feel it as it went cold. It would drip into her open mouth, and she'd taste it.

She'd know what he'd done and come at him with electric knives.

He needed to wipe it off, quickly, and it needed to be done in a way that wouldn't wake her. He reached out, ready to scoop it from her breasts but stopped just short.

There was something different about her.

It was her nipples.

He was certain they'd never been purple before. He was sure they'd always been red. Actually, he knew this for certain, as he'd daydreamed about them for years.

He frowned, and his hand lingered over her chest. He hesitated before wiping the pearlescent liquid away, with light fingers.

Her flesh was colder than normal. He had rubbed her back and stomach many times and knew she shouldn't be this cold.

With a ruffled brow, he looked at her face.

Her mouth was wide open.

His white stuff was dripping from her nose, into the gaping hole.

She wasn't licking her lips; she wasn't moving her hands to wipe it away. She wasn't moving at all.

His hands were clammy, and there was a different crawling in his crotch. This one penetrated his stomach. The horrible feeling he'd had climbing the stairs was back, only this time it was a thousand times worse.

He recognised it as panic.

A deep-rooted panic.

His legs went weak, and he was suddenly cold. Then he was far too hot, then suddenly freezing again. A warm, wet feeling crawled down his legs as his bladder opened, allowing the foul smelling, dark liquid to flow freely. He barely even noticed it as his eyes were fixated on her open mouth and the dripping white stuff that was now running down her cheek onto the grey pillow beneath her.

His legs buckled, and he stumbled.

He only knew he'd fallen when his face splashed into the warm puddle, and the sudden pain in his knees.

Then his world turned black.

Zola

4.

IT WAS THE dream again. Only this time, it was vivid. He could feel, he could smell. This time there were colours, horrible, bright colours. And tastes.

That was the worst part.

He was once again in the centre of a circle. The room was dark. The only illumination was a dim flickering light, issuing from the clusters of candles scattered all around. The smell of melting wax was prevalent in the air, but there was something else too, something familiar, something making his mouth water.

Then it came to him.

It was the same smell from the jar he had hidden underneath his bed.

It was the white stuff.

Only this was heavier than in the jar. This was stronger, wetter, if there was such a thing as a physical stink, this was it. He could taste it in the back of his throat. It lingered, all white, salty, fishy. He liked it, and he hated it, detested it equal measures.

He was naked, and he was freezing cold. His rolls of flab and the covering of the thick coarse hair that grew all over his body was doing nothing to keep Jack Frost's nips at bay. There was a wind blowing from somewhere, he didn't know where, but it was strong, with icy blades hiding within it, the tips of the icicle lashes were sharp enough to pierce his flesh. The wind was strong enough to move him. It blew him around the circle of hooded figures who were surrounding him, yet it wasn't enough to snuff the candles.

Each robed figure had their face covered, but he knew them. He recognised their auras. Ugly, black impressions, like dark clouds that threatened bad weather hovered around each figure. The clouds were so dark that the dim light from the candles couldn't penetrate them. As he was blown from side to side, the figures' robes blew open, revealing naked, twisted and knotted bodies beneath.

Half of them were men, the other half were like his mother, but with one stark difference.

They were all sporting huge erections.

As he was blown back and forth, their stiff *thinguses* were thrust into his face. Whenever he opened his mouth to scream, a *thingus* was forced deep into his open mouth. As he gagged, gasping for breath, he looked up. The figure who's cock was deep within him removed his hood.

His abuser revealed himself.

It was his father.

Or at least he thought it was his father, as he'd forgotten his face. It had been so long since he'd seen him, but he had *the impression* it was him.

The wind whipped again and blew him towards another *thingus*, and the exact same thing happened. The stinking cock was thrust deep into his open mouth. Spittle dripped from his chin as the foul-tasting appendage clogged his oesophagus. The face of his father glared down at him again, grinning, grinding, enjoying what he was doing.

Again, the wind took him. This time it pushed him towards one of the naked women. Again, her cock was forced between his unwilling lips. As the hood fell back, he saw the face of his mother, but as a much younger woman. Her beautiful face was laughing as she grabbed the back of his head and pushed her *thingus* as deep down his throat it would go.

His gag reflex kicked in, and he vomited. Hot bile mixed with cheese sauce that she had coated his steaks with dripped down the thick shaft of her cock, but still she pushed deeper.

Vomit and salty cheese were all he could taste, all he could smell, as erection after erection was forced into him, lancing him, using him.

All he could hear was the wind and the laughter of his parents whispering over it.

He was blown around the circle, fellating one shadowy figure of his father after another, intermingled with his mother for good measure.

All of them were moaning, rolling their heads, laughing. All of them were enjoying him.

It got so that he could no longer tell the difference from one dick to another, there were that many.

Then the wind died.

Rough hands pushed him back into the centre of the circle. The gang of shadowy figures gathered around him, all of them with their stiff dicks in their hands, all of them doing the thing he liked to do when his mother was in the bath, rubbing their hands up and down their shafts.

'Do you remember this, Gordon?' one of his fathers hissed. 'Do you remember me doing this to you? Me and all my friends? Do you?'

He wanted to shake his head, he wanted to tell him that he didn't remember it, that it never happened to him, but he couldn't. Something was stopping him.

'Now *you're* going to find how *you* like it,' one of his mothers hissed. He looked at her. 'Now it's you in the bath, and it's me rubbing *my* thingus.'

He looked at their faces. They were all staring down at him, their faces all caught in snarls. With lolling tongues and twitching legs, their hands were massaging their dicks in a perfect rhythm, moving faster and faster up and down their shafts.

Then, with a collective moan, their penises erupted.

All of them.

All at the same time.

He closed his eyes as thick warmth covered him. It spattered over his chest, his legs, his face.

It showed no signs of stopping anytime.

He opened his mouth, needing to breathe, but when he did, the warm slime slipped between his lips, into his mouth, down his throat.

It was warm, it was salty, and it was delicious.

It was cheese sauce.

The same his mother used to layer his steaks with.

There was so much of it that he was scared he might drown. The shadowy figures of his parents were all still thrashing their *thinguses*, all of them showering him in warm cheese sauce. It was up his nose, it clogged his throat, it stung his eyes, and blocked his ears.

The last thing he saw before his eyes closed over, before the cheese that smelt like his white stuff—but when it was warm—continued to cover him, was the decaying faces of his wanking parents.

He opened his eyes, hoping to wake up in the safety of his home, in his bed, but no… he was still there, still in the cheese filled circle. The shadowy, decaying figures were still leering over him. They had stopped tipping their sauce over him and were now covering each other in it. They were doing what he had seen some of the *gentlemen callers* do to his mother.

The floor was covered in cheese, the room was filling with it.

At first he was wading in it, then he was swimming in it. It was forcing its way into his mouth; his stomach was regurgitating it. He was drowning in vomit, dying in his favourite food, mixed with his own white stuff.

He began to swallow. It was delightful. Just like his mother made when. He licked the cheese from is arms, he cleaned his vomit from his fingers, and scooped mounds of cum into his waiting, salivating mouth.

As he swallowed, the familiar tingle between his legs began. He knew what that meant. His own *thingus* began to stiffen.

~~~~

He awoke on the floor in his mother's room. A thick dribble of saliva was tricking from his mouth, along his cheek, and pooling onto the sticky carpet beneath him.

His *thingus* was rock hard.

He twitched his hand. He could still move. *Good,* he thought. He closed his eyes, and surprisingly his dream came back to him. He gripped himself, between his legs, relishing the feel of it between his sweat lined fingers. He squeezed and pulled at it.

A few moments later, he was happily sucking on his fingers again. *Gordon Cakes,* he thought as he sat up.

Delicious!

Zola

5.

THE REST OF the day was spent on the couch. He used the threadbare throw that was over the back of it to keep himself warm. It wasn't a cold day, but he couldn't stop shaking. Everything in his life, everything he knew and had taken for granted was now gone. It had been taken away from him, and he was alone.

It was the first time in his life he'd ever even considered being alone. His mother had always been there for him. She was the one who did the … *the what?* he asked himself. *The stuff,* was all he could think of.

Suddenly, he realised that he didn't know how to make his mother's special cheese steaks, or her fantastic broth. Biting his cheeks, he got up on shaky legs and plodded his way into the kitchen.

He stood in the entrance, looking around him.

Everything felt alien to him.

He could see the cooker, and he knew how that worked. There was a large refrigerator in the corner where he knew his mother kept the pre-

prepared steaks and the broth, but he'd recently heard her mumbling about needing more supplies.

More supplies usually meant *gentleman callers*. All he knew about that was he had to stay out of the way when they came.

He didn't think he had the special skills, or what it took to bring *gentlemen callers* back to the house.

He hoped there was something inside the refrigerator. The realisation that he was hungry had just hit home. His stomach was literally crying out for food, it squelched and grumbled a chorus, and he felt sicker with every note of it. He rushed to the tall appliance and almost pulled the door of it off, in his haste to see what was in there. He took a step back as a dense cloud of slow-moving flies exited their chilled prison. The ones still able to fly were fat, sluggish, and slow. The other, not so lucky ones just fell out, onto the dirty lino, covering his bare feet. He smiled as the flying ones passed him. He opened his mouth, allowing some to fly into his mouth. He crunched these bloated beasts between his rotting teeth, chewing on them. Sour juice filled his mouth as their bloated bodies popped, and he swallowed. His stomach thanked him for the sustenance, however meagre it was. It was a bitter meal, but it wasn't the first time he'd eaten the monsters that frequented his home.

As he swallowed, the wings and legs scratched his throat. He knew this wouldn't sustain him; it was merely a starter. He needed something more … substantial.

He waved the rest of the flies away and looked inside the refrigerator. There was only one thing in there. The sight of it should have made him flinch. It should have taken his breath away. It would have caused any normal person to run, screaming blue murder out of the house, and given them cause enough for therapy for the rest of their lives. Gordon wasn't normal, and what was in there, he'd seen a hundred times before.

It was a human head.

It was standing in a plastic bowl that was collecting the juices that dripped from its rotting features. Crusted red, pink, yellows, and purples adorned the bowl. There were also large black clumps where some of the flies had died, obliviously happily, in the head nectar. He didn't exactly know what do with it, but he'd watched his mother carve them up before, cooking the strips on the stove.

Thinking nothing of it, he reached in and lifted the head out of the bowl by the hair. A strip tore away with a wet ripping sound and the head dropped back into the bowl. Its momentum rolled it out of the refrigerator and onto the floor, taking the bowl of juice with it. As it fell, he tried to catch it, and the cold liquid spilled over his chest, down his legs, and pooled around his feet.

He cursed and tutted.

Knowing there was only one thing for it, he got down on his hands and knees and licked the semi-congealed mess from the filthy floor.

It was cold, and it tasted like metal, but there was lumps in it that he had to crunch. He enjoyed those bits. When the head gravy was all lapped up, he removed clumps of dirt from his mouth while smacking his lips and licking at his moist whiskers. The juice, along with the flies, had been good, but it still wasn't enough. His stomach was still complaining. It had taken a taste, dipped its beak so to speak, and was now demanding more.

His eyes fell onto the head.

The head looked back at him.

He didn't recognise its face. But that didn't really mean anything to him, as he'd never recognised any of the heads he'd found in the refrigerator.

Its open eyes stared at him. There were thick, milky cataracts accusing him of things he hadn't done … not yet. The bald spot on the top of its head where the hair had torn away was oozing. A thick yellow grease was forming over the wound. He leaned forwards and licked it. It was almost as bitter as the flies – almost. He tightened his lips and reached for it. He inserted two fingers into the wound and scooped out a mound of the yellow gunk. He sniffed at it.

It smelt horrible.

Gordon shrugged.

He'd smelt worse.

He put the glob into his mouth and sucked the rest from his fingers.

He'd been wrong, it was worse than the flies.

A lot worse.

It was so sour it made him want to spit. It was tough to swallow, but as his mouth was now filled with spit, he saw no point in wasting any of the goodness. Wiping tears from his eyes, he swallowed while eyeing the rest of the head, suspiciously.

He'd watched when his mother took these and put them in the big metal pot on the stove. He'd watched her fill the pot with water and boil it all up. She added salt and pepper, these he knew, and other stuff that was dry and green. He didn't know what those were, but he was ready to experiment.

He picked up the head, careful not to rip it anymore. It was difficult to grip as the thing must have been in the refrigerator for some time and it had gone soft and wet. His fingers squished through the rotting skin, poking holes in the cheeks. From each hole he made there was another release of flies, and an outpouring of maggots. The sight of these little wriggling worms made his mouth water again. He'd eaten them before and knew they were much sweeter than the flies they eventually became.

He licked his lips.

'No, Gordon,' he chastised himself. 'Save them for the broth.'

Holding the head out before him, at full arm's length, he made his way to the cooker. His full attention had been on his prize, rather than where he was stepping, so he didn't notice the residue of juice that had spilt from the bowl. As his bare foot stepped into it, he slipped right out from underneath him. As he fell, he juggled the head, comically passing it from one hand to the other, all the while trying to keep himself upright.

He failed on both counts.

As he finally fell to the wet floor with splat, the head went flying in the air.

It hit the floor with a splat, almost as loud as his was. As it hit the linoleum, it split into three parts. It reminded him of a smashed pumpkin head that had been left out long after Halloween was over. The contents spilled from the cracks—one on the side of the head, separating an ear from the rest of the face, another at the back of the head, where more of the yellow grease oozed from the exposed, cracked bone, and the third split the face in two.

A thick, discoloured, and bloated tongue lolled from one of the splits. He recoiled when he saw it, his arms and legs flailing as they tried to gain purchase on the slippery floor, as he attempted to push himself away from it. The tongue was moving! It looked like it was sending rude gestures to him. It wasn't until he backed himself into the wall that he realised his stupidity.

The tongue wasn't moving, it was just infested with maggots.

He laughed, a little nervous chuckle, while still keeping one eye on the mashed up head.

With an absurd sucking sound, a dripping eye popped out from its socket. The other had burst, dripping brown juice down the distorted face.

'Ruined,' he tutted, as he made his way slowly back to inspect the mess. 'Fucking ruined!' He looked around the room, hoping his mother would be there, looking at him with a disapproving face. She hated *potty language,* as she called it. But of course, she wasn't there, she was upstairs, in her bed, still very much dead.

He looked at the split head and the inordinate amount of flies already gathered upon it, sending head-party invitations to the rest of their colleagues.

He sighed.

A clump of flesh peeled off and fell to the floor.

The flies followed it.

Careful not to slip on the slime again, he made his way to the cutlery drawer and selected a spoon. He sat, cross legged, the linoleum cold on his fleshy behind, but he didn't mind, he had bigger fish to fry than cold balls.

He took the spoon to the smashed head.

He prised open the crack at the back, just wide enough for him to fit the spoon inside.

As he didn't want to get hair in his meal, he detested the feel of hair in his mouth, he knew the crack wouldn't be wide enough. Putting the spoon on the floor, he eased his fingers into the head. He looked at the ear that was hanging loose and wondered what that would taste like.

That's for later, he thought as he pulled the crack wider. It gave way easier than he thought it might, and a sloppy grey chunk flew out. He watched it slip down the off-white of the refrigerator door.

It looked kind of off to him, reminding him of the yellow ooze he'd fingered out of the wound earlier. Although his stomach was still grumbling, demanding to be noticed, to be fed, the festered brain morsel didn't tempt him.

The face was hanging loose on one half of the head. It reminded him of the dwarves from the cartoon he and his mother had enjoyed when he was younger. This made him smile, and he attempted to whistle the jaunty little tune. He couldn't quite get it right, but the memory was a good one.

The wound was covered with hair, as green, yellow, and grey filth tricking from it.

'Eat it, Gordon!'

It was his mother's voice.

He turned to see where she was, overjoyed that she wasn't dead. But then he realised she would be angry with him for spraying his *white stuff* over her face. 'I'm sorry, M ...' he started.

There was no one there.

He knew there wouldn't be.

When someone stopped moving, like mother's *gentlemen callers* stopped, they never moved again.

Reluctantly, he turned back to his meal. He picked the spoon up from the floor. He sucked on it, just to get the grime off it, then plunged it into the head. This time it went in easily.

He grinned at the squelching sound.

The spoon came out with a mound of jellied matter on it. He grimaced. *Pretend it's one of mother's cheese steaks,* he thought, closing his eyes and opening his mouth to receive the offering.

It was cold, it was bitter, but it wasn't as bad as he was expecting. *It just needs a little bit of ...* he stopped this thought short. 'Gordon, you clever boy,' he muttered. He stood, shaking off the pins and needles in his legs, and went to the fridge. He looked at the little bit of brain had slid down to the bottom of the door. He thought of scooping it up and popping it in his mouth anyway, but pushed that thought away, his new idea was a lot more exciting, a lot more palatable. Ignoring the chunk, he opened the door, he looked at the drawers at the bottom and smiled.

There it was, exactly what he was looking for.

The bottom drawer was filled with packets of cheese.

She always bought a lot of it, normally after a *gentleman caller* had been over. There was roughly half of the usual supply left. It was more than enough for what he had in mind. He gave an inward cheer and removed a chunk from one of the packets. Gorgonzola, it read on the packet. It was one of the few words he could read.

It's my cheese, he thought with a smile.

He pulled at the plastic coating, relishing the aroma as it came away in his hands. It was a lot nicer than the smell of the head, but so were a lot of things.

He took the chunk and rolled it in his hands, softening it. He plunged his spoon back into the head and removed another jellied mass. He crumbled the softened cheese over it before taking a big sniff.

Instantly, his mouth watered.

Without any preamble, he stuffed the spoon into his mouth.

'Better,' he mumbled as rotten brains, mixed with mouldy cheese, dripped from his mouth into his beard.

It *was* better, but it was no cheese steak.

~~~~

With his stomach full and the stranger's head hollowed out on the floor—complete with an ear with a bite taken out of it but spat back on the floor, it was nowhere near as nice as it looked, he thought it might taste like bacon—he climbed the stairs, ready for a nap.

As he passed his mother's room, he couldn't help but have a quick glance inside, just to see if she had moved.

She hadn't.

This saddened him.

He loved her and would miss her, but most of all, he was going to miss her cheese steaks.

6.

A FEW DAYS passed, but his hunger didn't. He awoke with a sickeningly empty feeling in the pit of his stomach.

'Mother,' he shouted. 'I'm starving.'

He was about to peel his flabby torso from his threadbare bed and go and look for her, when reality hit him. *Mother's dead,* he thought. *She can't make me breakfast.* This saddened him for two reasons. Never again would he be able to talk to his beautiful mother, or see her lovely smile, and never again would he get to eat one of her delicious cheese steaks.

As his bare feet touched the festering carpet, he smacked his lips together. The first thing he could taste was the cheesy brains he'd eaten for the last three days. The remains of them were languishing in his filthy beard. He rubbed his face and what flakes came off in his hands, he quickly popped into his mouth. His meals had gotten worse each time he'd sampled them, and the thought of scraping around inside that stinking head again today, trying to find some of the evil tasting mess that was not too rotten to eat, saddened him even more than the thought of his mother lying dead in the next room.

I could just eat the cheese, he thought, trying to convince himself that cheese alone would be enough to satisfy the desolate feeling he had in the pit of his stomach, and in his soul.

He dragged his huge, hairy body out of the bed and stretched. The stink of his grimy flesh was lost on him, it had been for years if the truth be told. He reached around and scratched at his scabby behind, first removing the crusts that lined the crease of his crack and eating them, then delving deeper, inserting two fingers to the first knuckles to scratch at the itch inside the hole itself. He looked at his beige fingers and sniffed them. He then scraped the greasy film underneath his fingernails along the ridge of his few remaining teeth. He swilled this scum around his mouth before swallowing.

All this did was wake his stomach, making it start its terrible song of longing once again.

He needed to eat something substantial, and he needed to do it soon.

He passed his mother's room and dared another peep inside, as had become his morning, and evening, ritual. She was becoming difficult to see due to the influx of flies hovering over her, but he wanted to make sure she hadn't gotten up in the middle of the night and disappeared.

Dead or alive, he wanted her with him.

She was still there.

A sad smile passed over his features before he continued along the landing. Suddenly he stopped. He looked back towards her door. A feeling engulfed him; it had started as little more than a tingle down below, but he knew exactly what it was. The sensation wanted him to go and take another look at her. More specifically, her breasts. He longed to see the deep veins, the bluish hue of her skin, and her purple nipples.

His *thingus* was getting hard again just at the thought of her. His heartbeat was up, and he was chewing at the skin on the inside of his mouth. He closed his eyes, clenched his fists, exhaled, then pushed on downstairs, damming his thoughts.

The flies downstairs were worse than upstairs. He had to wave them away even before he was on the last step because he couldn't see where he was going. If he fell and bashed his head, there wouldn't be anyone to come running to help him. The only person, the only woman, he could have ever relied on was upstairs, lying unmoving in her bed.

Another thought occurred to him. He didn't know where this one came from, but he hoped it wasn't from his own head, as it would have confirmed to him that he was going crazy. It might have come from his stomach, however. *Yeah, that's where it's come from,* he thought. *My stomach is talking to me now.*

He thought about his mother's cheese steaks.

After three days of eating some stranger's head, a head that had been languishing in the refrigerator for God only knew how long, he was craving something else, something tasty.

He wanted cheese steaks.

His mother's cheese steaks.

'But Mother's dead,' he said aloud to no one. His eyes darted towards the kitchen, where the cloud of flies was most dense. 'I'm all out of cheese steaks,' he continued. 'But I'm not out of cheese …'

Zola

The stink from his mother's bedroom filled the house. It was something he was able to get used to; he'd smelt the, not so sweet, scent of death most of his life. Even though it could get pretty thick now and then, it was a smell he associated with his mother, and with food. He looked back up the fly-infested stairs. He couldn't see her room from where he was, but he knew she was up there.

His mouth watered.

Could I?

He thought he could.

Crunching his way through the fat flies, some of them far too fat to fly so they scurried around the floor, he made his way into the kitchen. Being careful not to slip on the grime covered floor again, he diverted his eyes from what was left of the head, lying in three hollowed out pieces, in the centre of the room. This wasn't because it was a purple, rotting husk with a bite out of one of its ears, but because of the nasty taste it left in his mouth.

'Dirty thing,' he hissed as he opened the refrigerator.

Inside there was cheese.

Quite a few packets of the stuff.

He loved it. He always had. It made his steaks that much nicer.

He grabbed a packet and ripped open the plastic. The cheese was slightly wet inside. His mother had always said she'd rather eat sweaty cheese, as she put it, than overly chilled as it brought out the flavour.

He happened to agree with her.

In the drawer where she kept the cutlery, he found the electric knife. He picked it up, his eyes widening as he examined the sharp, serrated edges. He'd always wanted to have a go of it, but she'd never allowed him. 'You'll cut your fingers off,' she'd warned. A tear welled in his eyes on hearing her voice in his head. With a wry smile, he attached the dirty blades into the device as he'd seen her do on a thousand occasions. Nodding, he made his way through the kitchen.

He grimaced as his foot went cold. He looked down and saw what he'd stepped in. The dark, empty eye-sockets of the stranger's head stared blankly up at him from two separate parts of the ruined face. Briefly, he wondered who he had been, then shrugged. He didn't care. He lifted his foot from the sticky floor and wiped the squishy residue from between his toes. Absently, he sucked the filth from his fingers as he made his way out of the kitchen, towards the stairs.

Towards his mother's room.

~~~~

The smell was heavy, it felt physical, like he could have cut through it with the electric knives, but it wasn't wholly unpleasant. It made his stomach sing again. It sang a song of cheese steaks to him, only voiced in whale song. His eyes lit as he looked at the electric knife. He wasn't sure how to use it, but he'd seen her work it, and it didn't look too hard.

He plugged it into a socket in reaching distance to the bed and pressed the button. The two blades burst into life, rubbing against each other, creating the perfect cutting tool. He pulled back the sheets covering his mother's torso and looked at her. She was still in the same position he'd found her. The only difference was her skin; it was darker, greyer. The flesh on her face seemed to have shrunk, pulling her features back. The flies were eating into her eyes and crawling in and out of her nostrils and mouth. He didn't mind that; he had no intention of doing anything with those parts of her anyway.

There was also a spreading brown stain around her backside. He looked to see what could have been the cause and saw there had been leakage from her bottom. It still looked wet. He shook his head, a wistful smile crawled over his face. 'Oh, Mother,' he fussed. 'Look at what you've done. You've gone and dirtied yourself,' he chuckled.

That was when his eyes fell on her purple nipples.

The familiar tingle in his *thingus* stirred again.

He looked around the room, his guilt making him check no one had snuck into the house to spy on him doing what he was about to do.

There was no one there.

He was totally alone.

Who's going to know?

Putting the knife down, he reached between his legs and began to stroke his *thingus*. His tongue peeped out of his mouth with every stroke, accompanied by a deep breath. His eyes were concentrating on her blue/grey breasts. He pushed himself to go a little faster, enjoying the rapid beating of his heart. He looked at her fly-infested open mouth; her jaw had slackened, widening the maw of blackness.

Would it fit?

The thought was exciting. It was something he'd never thought of before, something completely new to him.

He leaned over, onto his tiptoes, and pushed his *thingus* towards her mouth. His breathing was rapid, shallow, the rhythm was totally irregular as he waved the flies away and guided his dick between her purple lips.

This was new, and it was a game changer in his opinion. It took rubbing himself to a whole new level. Even though it was cold, it was wet, and that allowed him to slip it in easier. It didn't take long for the feeling in his toes to start, and the moan that escaped him set off a chain reaction.

A beautiful chain reaction.

The tingle crept up to his knees, then his legs, and as he flexed his meaty calves, as his *thingus* spat his sweet white stuff into her mouth.

It spat and spat. It continued to spit. There was more of his white stuff than he'd seen in a long time. A lot more.

With his breath returning to normal and an itchy wet drip dangling from the tip of his cock, he leaned back, wiping the sweat from his brow.

He swallowed, trying to get his breathing back to something resembling normality when he saw his white stuff dribbling from her open mouth. He leaned in intending to wipe it away, but as he got closer, he caught a whiff of her sweet decay, it was mingling with the *white* smell of his stuff.

It was like nothing he had ever smelt before in his life.

It was- dare he say it- beautiful.

He leaned closer. Her face inches away from his. He couldn't help himself; buoyed by his physical proximity to her, to the woman he'd loved all of his life, he kissed her.

His hairy, chapped lips met with her cold, wet ones.

He'd read books, and seen on some TV shows, that when two people loved each other very much, they would kiss with their tongues. So, because he did love her, *had loved her,* very much, this was what he wanted to do.

He had never kissed a girl with his tongue before, and it excited him. Even though he'd only just spurted from is *thingus,* he could feel another twinge in it. Licking the scum that lined what was left of his teeth, bit his top lip, and moved closer.

The smell of his *white stuff* was intoxicating. He wanted to taste it now. He longed to lick it off her lips and savour it.

Is this a new kind of Gordon Cake?

He slipped his tongue into her open mouth. A few flies flew out of hers, and into his. Normally, he wouldn't have minded this, but it came as a shock, and he moved his head back, allowing the fat black beasts their freedom. His *thingus* was totally hard again, and he moved back into her. His tongue slipped back inside her foul mouth. It probed around her decaying, mouth. It licked her slimy tongue, her teeth, the insides of her cheeks, and finally, the roof of her mouth.

He tasted everything.

It was nice.

It was more than nice; it was the best thing he'd ever experienced.

His *thingus* throbbed as he licked and sucked his own white stuff out of her. It was better than any Gordon Cake he'd ever tasted before. The throb in his cock was sending sensations all around his body, as if his heart had moved out of his chest and was now conducting its business from the tip of this *thingus*. He stopped it from spurting by pulling away and squeezing its swollen tip.

When it was under control, he turned his attentions back to her.

With his breathing speeding up again and his body shivering from all the adrenaline currently pumping through his veins, he wrapped his hand around the back of her head and pulled her closer. It was a tough job, as he had to tear away strips of skin that had stuck to the pillow and the sheets beneath her. But he managed it without too much damage.

He held her in this romantic embrace, looking at the face he loved the most in the whole world. He held her like this for a few more heartbeats before he moved his own face closer and inserted his tongue deeper into her mouth than he had before.

He sucked again, wanting to get all his white stuff out of her.

It was delicious, salty, and still a little warm, but it was nowhere near as good as the cheese on his steaks. He licked her whole mouth clean, before sucking again, a little harder this time. Something dislodged from within her and came up out of her mouth. He had no idea what it could be, but it was thick, wet, and extremely bitter.

His *thingus* wilted almost instantly.

He pulled away, wiping his beard, which was wet with his own white stuff. He wiped it and looked at his hand. There was something else on his dirty hand. Something dark. Maybe it was red, maybe it was black, but whatever it was, it didn't taste nice. He spat it on the floor and looked at it.

He thought it was her tongue. It was bloated, purple, and it was wriggling with maggots, just like the other head, the one in the kitchen.

A thick black goo was dripping from her mouth now. He stuck out his own tongue and wiped it with his hands, raking his fingernails down it, attempting to get whatever it was off it.

I won't be doing that again, he thought.

Although the moment the thought was out of his head, he couldn't guarantee he would live up to the promise.

Before the tongue had come off, it had been pretty nice.

He leaned in close and tried to close her mouth, wiping the black goo with disdain. 'I love you mother,' he whispered.

Sucking in a deep breath, he picked up the electric knives and pressed the button again. The noise was loud in the quiet room, it was the loudest thing he'd heard in a while, and it startled him. He put his hands to his head, attempting to block the ugly noise, and the rusty blades bit deep into the back of his hand.

Screaming, he dropped the knife on the floor, narrowly missing his toes. It stopped making the noise, and for a short while, he just stood there, looking at it, holding his hand.

He looked at the cheese on the bed, and his stomach growled again. Even through the stinging, his stomach wanted the cheese steaks, and it wanted them now.

His hand was dripping blood, and he panicked. Blood had never been an issue to him, he'd seen a fair bit in his time, but he didn't think he'd ever seen so much of his own. There was a discarded pair of his mother's panties on the floor. It looked like they had once been white. Now, however, they were grey, with a multi-coloured haze over the gusset. As he picked them up, they were stiff, and he had to crunch them to make them pliable. He sniffed the crotch and grinned, despite the pain in his hand. The smell reminded him of her, and that made him happy.

Some of the colour peeled away from the gusset, and he couldn't help but pick it off and eat it. It didn't taste as good as it smelt, but it was still a little bit of *her* that he didn't have before.

He wrapped the panties around his bleeding hand, and it stemed the flow, for now at least.

He picked up the knife with his good hand and pressed the button. The blades sprung back into life, but this time, they didn't scare him. He pouted as he looked at his mother. She was on her side; her hip was sticking up in the air. He licked his lips. *There,* he thought, admiring the blue fleshy mound. He angled the moving blades towards her and applied pressure.

In his mind, she screamed, she shouted and pleaded for him to stop, just as he'd heard some of her *gentleman callers* do. But in reality, she didn't do anything.

She didn't even move.

The blades sliced into her putrid meat as if they were hot, and she had been made of butter. He was able to shave off a thick slice. He put the blades down, careful not to cut himself again. He reached over and removed the cheese he'd brought from its packet. As he tore off a chunk, his blood dripped from the panties onto the slab of dairy, but he didn't mind. He took the sliver of his mother and wrapped it around his dairy delight. He then sat back and regarded his meal. Some unidentifiable grime dripped from it. It was black and thick, but on the whole, it looked a lot more appetising than the brains he'd been eating for the last few days.

He put it to his mouth and took a bite.

The flesh was rubbery. It was wet, and cold. It took a little work, but eventually, he was able to force his bad teeth to bite through it, getting to the cheesy goodness in the centre.

He chewed and nodded.

A 'Hammam,' escaped him. *This is good,* he thought. *Not as good as she made them. But now they are made* from *her.* It seemed fitting somehow. Like it was something she would have approved; of that, he was certain.

The meat was tough and difficult to chew. He needed something to soften it up. He remembered that mother sometimes put her steaks into flavoured water overnight. 'To tenderise it, and to give it that little bit of extra taste,' she'd say with a smile. *That's what I need to do.*

He finished this meal, savouring the cheese, with the blood from his cut hand adding just a little bit of extra salt.

He was enjoying himself; it was fun using his brain.

There was a plastic box in the corner of the room that was loaded with junk. He spilled the contents onto the floor and looked inside. 'Perfect,' he muttered. He cut two more steaks from her. He'd thought about slicing up her breasts, as they looked like they would be nice meat, but he stopped himself. He had selfish *reasons* for keeping them intact for as long as he could. After wrapping the slices around two more chunks of cheese, he went to find something to marinade them in.

Search as he might, he couldn't find anything he thought would make them softer and tastier like mother had done.

He was at a loss. He had never marinaded anything before and had no idea what was required. When he'd watched her do it, she had put stuff into water to make it dark.

'But what was it?' he asked the empty house.

The house answered back.

'You need something soft to pack them in,' it whispered. 'Something soft and sweet. You know where you can find that.'

A grin passed over his face as his eyes lit up. He knew exactly what was needed, and where to find it.

Right now, there were two places.

The first one was obvious. He remembered the moment he'd pulled the covers away from her body, and saw she'd dirtied herself.

He hadn't thought anything of it at the time, after all, *he* did it all the time. But right now, he thought it was exactly what he needed.

The second place was the toilet. That was always full of brown water. *That must have been what she used,* he thought.

Perfect.

'I'll pack them first,' he was excited at the prospect of his new recipe. 'I'll wrap the steaks in her dirty, then get the gravy from the toilet.'

Grinning at his ingenuity, a sad moment passed through him, as he wished his mother had been here. She would have been so proud of him. He scoffed when he realised that he'd gotten his wish. She *was* here, *of course she is*. He rolled his eyes and continued his work.

He yanked the blankets all the way off her corpse and found what he was looking for around the back. The spreading brown stain was still there. It had gotten a little bigger since he'd last looked at it. It looked like both liquids and now some of the solids had leaked from her. It was now thick and a little lumpy.

He tutted.

The flies feasting on the sweet brown mess protested as he swished his hands at them. They flew, buzzing angrily, circling around his head. He hardly noticed them as he concentrated on the stain. He twisted his mouth as he regarded it. He didn't think there would be enough there to cover the steaks. He cupped the brown clumps in his hands and dumped them into the box. The smell was sickly sweet, like when he'd had an upset stomach. It coated his nostrils, masking her decay, but again, it was something he could handle.

He liked it.

He was used to it.

He slapped the thick brown matter around the two steaks in the plastic box, packing them in as thick as he could, nodding as he regarded his handywork.

However, no matter how hard he tried, there just wasn't enough to cover the slivers of flesh.

He looked at the bed; there was very little left, certainly not enough for what his requirements.

His eyes followed the beige stain as it trickled out from between the crack of her bottom. He reached over and pulled her cheeks back.

A cloying stink issued from it, one that cemented itself into his nostrils. It was like nothing he had ever smelt before; it was so bad that it affected even him. The stink wasn't the only thing to come from between those cheeks. A wad of brown matter fell from the small hole between the cheeks, splatting onto the wet mattress.

He grinned; it was exactly what he needed. He scooped it up and packed it around the steaks.

There still wasn't enough to fully marinade them.

He pulled her cheeks back again. This time there was no splatter. He held his breath and leaned in, peering into the small, relaxed hole where the brown stuff had dripped from. An idea came to him then. He inserted two fingers from his uninjured hand and slathered them with spit. He them slipped the wet fingers into the hole. The escape of air was horrible, even by his standards. As he pulled his fingers out, a slurry of filth came with them. It was so bad that he had to step away from the source of the foul stench, holding his hand beneath his nostrils to mask it, not realising that the reek would be on his fingers too.

He gagged, but the stench of his hands wasn't as bad as what was coming out of her anal cavity.

After a few moments, the stink had either expelled itself or he'd gotten used to it. He decided to lean in for another inspection as he'd seen more of the brown matter leaking from it.

Buoyed by this, he sucked on the same fingers and re-inserted them. This time, the escaping air was tolerable, but only just. He pushed them in as deep as they would go, way past his knuckles. He flexed them, rummaging inside for any of brown stuff that might be languishing inside.

It was cold inside her, but it was wet and soft. As he pulled his fingers back out, another slurry of shit flowed from the hole.

Bingo. He grinned, packing his steaks in the newfound resource.

Zola

Happy with that the covering would now cover the steaks, he carried the box into the bathroom.

The toilet hadn't been washed for weeks, maybe months, but probably years, he didn't know, nor did he care. The flush hadn't worked in a while either, so as he'd pooped, and taken a tinkle, it had been piling up. A smooth tip was sticking out of the brown water, looking like a shit iceberg. Only a small percentage of it protruded from the gravy, the majority was below.

He knew this from the TV. *It's a shit-burg,* he thought with a chuckle.

Without hesitation, he took a glass that was next to the sink, reached into the bowl, and filled it with the sludge.

He had used his cut hand for this, without thinking, and sucked in a sharp breath as the cold, dirty water penetrated the panties, and seeping into his wound.

Her tried again, this time with his good hand. The brown stuff squished between his fingers, and he laughed at how strange it felt.

The smell was worse than in the bedroom, and the flies protested again at his intrusion into their domain, but he paid none of it any mind, he was enjoying himself too much now. He poured the brown water over the steaks, covering them completely.

When the box was mostly full, he looked at his food parcels, proud of what he'd accomplished here this morning.

But most of all, he was proud that *she* would be proud of him.

He licked his hand clean of the residue.

It tastes like cheese, but with nuts in.

He unwrapped the wet panties from his stinging hand and wrung them out, marvelling at how much brown water they had absorbed. He re-covered his still fresh wound before carrying the box to the kitchen. With his head held high and a pleased grin, he placed it in the refrigerator. 'That'll do. One for dinner, and one for supper,' he said, rubbing his hands on his naked legs, leaving brown swathes down each thigh.

His injured hand was throbbing, but he ignored it. He went back upstairs, ready for a lie down, and a nap, where he could dream about his dinner.

~~~~

The meal was not as good as he'd anticipated.

The meat was still tough, and the smell of shit overpowered the taste of the cheese.

He tried both steaks, both with the same result.

'What a waste,' he hissed, placing his half-finished meal on the couch next to him. Although the flies disagreed with his verdict and wasted no time finding the treat. He seethed as he watched them revelling over his inedible meal. 'At least someone's enjoying it,' he muttered.

He went to bed still hungry, his cut hand swollen, red, and throbbing.

7.

HE WOKE THE next morning with an idea. It might have come to him in a dream, or he might just be a genius, but it was something he thought could work.

He'd been thinking about when he'd kissed his mother with his tongue after he'd sprayed her mouth with his white stuff. *It had been salty, and sweet too,* he reasoned. *All it needed was cheese.*

He had an idea how to make his steaks perfect.

He jumped out of bed and waddled down to the kitchen. He rummaged through all the drawers before finding exactly what he'd been looking for. He grasped a few of them, a packet of cheese from the cupboard, and shuffled back upstairs.

He was excited. He knew this was going to work, and the plus side was that he would enjoy himself in the process too. It combined two of his most favourite things in the world.

Ignoring the incessant throb in his hand, he hurried into his mother's room and removed her blankets. His wide eyes drank in the sight of her flaccid, blue tinged breasts. Her purple, now almost black nipples did their trick, and he felt his *thingus* twinge.

He grinned as he began to stroke it with his good hand, careful not to go too fast. He needed control this time.

While he stroked himself, he tore open the packet of cheese he'd brought with him with his teeth and bit off a sizable chunk. He chewed it but was careful not to swallow.

It was all part of his plan.

He then took one of the plastic straws he'd found in the drawer. He looked at the end and squeezed it, making it thinner. He then took another straw and attached it to the other end, and then another. Before long, he had one long straw that would be the perfect tool for what he had in mind.

Orange drool dripped from his mouth as he grinned, but it caught in his beard, and he was able to suck it back into his mouth. He didn't want to lose any, he needed as much of it as he could get for this to work.

With his mouth closed, he sat on the bed next to his dead mother. He pulled back the skin around his stiff *thingus* and ran his finger around the ridge, collecting all the white stuff that lay hidden here. He slipped it into his mouth. *The more the merrier,* he thought. He took the straw, and closing his eyes and tightening his lips, he slid a thinned-out end into the slit in the head of his cock. He took a sharp breath through his nose—so as not to spill any cheese. It smarted, no, it stung, a lot more than he'd expected. He closed his eyes, enduring the pain, and pushed the straw a little further in. Once the initial discomfort had subsided, he was left with a stinging, scratchy itch as the plastic slipped deeper down his shaft. This part was nowhere near as bad as he thought it was going to be, in fact, it

118

was rather nice. It distracted him from the throbbing in his puffy, reddened hand.

He slipped the other end of the straw into his mouth, careful not to let any of the liquefied cheese seep out.

Piercing his lips, he dribbled the cheese and spit cocktail into the straw and blew lightly, allowing it to slide down inside his erection.

It was an odd feeling having something go *into* his *thingus,* but again, it wasn't unpleasant.

When his mouth was empty and his cock was bloated with mushed dairy, he removed the straw, once again inhaling a sharp breath. He had to wait a moment for his head to stop spinning when the plastic slipped out of the little eye. He marvelled at the orange liquid seeping from the tip, pooling around his retracted foreskin.

He looked at his dead mother's breasts and began to stroke himself again. His cock felt strange, the thick liquid was shifting and squishing inside the shaft. His fingers could push it, moving it up and down.

He needed to time this right.

He braved his bad hand to work his *thingus* while his good one reached down to her dead body. He inserted three fingers into her mouth. Then a naughty thought occurred to him as he stroked himself harder. He moved his hand down the purple flesh of her chest, tracing his fingers over the splitting skin of her stomach.

It was the first time he'd thought of touching her here.

Well, that's what he tried to convince himself, when really, he'd wanted to touch between her legs for a long time, even before she was dead, but he had never dared.

The fact that she didn't have a *thingus* fascinated him, and he was desperate to know what was down there. Slowly, his fingers slipped between the cold flab of her thighs. It was freezing down there, and it was wet and sticky. Something was tickling his fingers. He didn't know if it was hair, flies, or even spiders. *Maybe it's all three,* he thought as his sore hand gripped his erection tighter.

Where her *thingus* should have been, there was a slit. He closed his eyes and slid two of his fingers inside it. It was clammy in there too, and something squishy touched him. It reminded him of the times his mother had made gravy, or custard, and left it to go cold, and a film had developed over the mixture. It also reminded him of when he inserted his fingers into her bottom to remove the old poop. Whatever it was, it was thick and clumpy, and there was a strange odour, it was like fish but also different, worse.

He gripped his *thingus* tighter and stroked faster. He removed his fingers and sniffed them. They were coated with a reddish jelly, and the fish stink coming from them reminded him of tins of salmon they'd had once, he'd enjoyed them on bread with best butter and vinegar. He licked the jelly off them. It was something new, something different. It tasted metallic, like licking a penny or a live battery. The new sensation set off the familiar chain reaction from his feet to his cheese loaded cock.

His knees began to buckle, and he knew exactly what was about to happen.

He gripped his screaming hand tighter around his shaft and let the feeling go.

He never really had a choice.

Zola

The explosion was beautiful.

Colours swam around him as he gushed. The feeling was like nothing he'd ever experienced before. The discharge was thicker than usual. It didn't spray like it normally did, but he managed to dribble it over the places he needed it to go.

It was thick, orange and white—and he thought there was a little red in there too. It covered her darkened split skin with precision.

When his head stopped swimming and he was steady on his feet again, he wiped his *thingus* and tasted his hand.

He rolled his eyes as he reeled in the taste sensation.

His mouth exploded with saliva.

It was quite simply *the* nicest things he had ever tasted in the whole of his life. It was so much better than the marinaded steaks, maybe even better than anything his mother had ever cooked for him.

He took the electric knife and wasted no time slicing into her flesh. He realised too late where he had sprayed her. It was her breasts. He hadn't wanted to cut them off, not yet anyway, but the thought of eating them now, slathered in his very own *Gordon's Special Sauce*, drove him crazy.

The fatty flesh cut away easily. He dropped the knife and picked up a chunk of the wet flesh. He savoured it, just for a moment, before stuffing it into his mouth.

He could taste it instantly. He had never had anything better in his mouth. It was softer than her hips had been, and the cheese mixed with his Gordon Cake mix and the blood from his wound, which was now badly swollen and turning a little bit green, was the perfect mix of salty goodness.

Without caring, he cut another chunk and gobbled it up as fast as he'd eaten the first. He leaned in and licked the remaining *Gordon's Special Sauce* from her last remaining breast, taking a little extra time to suck on the black, wet nipple. It was cold, but there was something about the feel of it covered in his sauce, his very own recipe, on his tongue that he couldn't explain. It was almost too good.

He stopped sucking as he felt her skin tear in his mouth, and he didn't want to choke on a nipple.

His stinging *thingus* was fully stiff again.

Time for more sauce, he thought, grinning, as he popped more cheese into his mouth.

~~~~

That night, he went to bed with a smile. He was content for the first time in what felt like a long time, since mother died at least. He'd eaten his fill and knew now there was something to look forward to in the morning.

His hand was still throbbing from the deep cut and was now so swollen that his fingers looked like little stubs and were difficult to bend. The wound was yellow, green, and brown, mostly from dried shit and congealed blood from cutting his mother up. He put his fingers in his mouth, attempting to sooth the ache.

It worked to a degree, and he flopped down, into a deep, dreamless sleep.

Zola

8.

HE WAS FREEZING.

He was roasting.

He felt sick.

He was starving.

His *thingus* was stinging. His bowels were bubbling. His hand was swollen, sending its agony shooting up and down, and all around his body.

He wanted to get up. He wanted to spit more cheese into his cock so he could spray it all over his mother's other tit, and eat it, but he didn't think he could move.

His stomach rumbled. It felt like wind was moving around his stomach, and with an effort, he lifted his flabby leg to let it escape. The movement made his brain spin, and sent a cold shiver through his fat, hairy body. A stream of hot, stinging fluid came with it, from both ends.

The stink was hideous.

At first, he thought it was milk that had gone off, or even a different kind of cheese, then he thought it might have been his dead mother coming for him, wanting her breasts back. It then became some unknown monster; one made of shit and maggots, smothered in his very own white stuff, and the contents of his special jar. All of it dripping from its arms, and its claws. Its head was the split head of the stranger in the refrigerator with his ear hanging off, with a bite taken out of it.

He opened his eyes and scanned the room, convinced the beast was there, ready to envelope him in its juices, to insert him into its relaxed asshole, and absorb there, leaving him to ferment for a thousand years.

At first, he couldn't see anything. His eyes were stinging and were filled with water. He had been brought up in squalor and filth for the whole of his life, but this was, by far, the worst thing he'd ever smelt.

His stomach flipped, and he retched.

A stream of thick vomit sluiced from his mouth. As vomit came out, the old vomit he'd done moments ago, slipped in. His beard was coated in it, his long sweaty hair, and the whole of his bed was too.

With the strain of vomiting, and trying not to swallow his old vomit, he forced out a squirt of shit from the other end, and the two liquids from polar end of his bulk met in the indentation his body made in the worn-out mattress.

He needed to get up, he needed to breathe, but he couldn't move. It wasn't just his hand that was puffy and bloated now, his whole arm was.

He couldn't move, he was stuck, like the world's pinkest hippopotamus, wallowing in its own filth.

He tried to push his bulk up, but his traitorous, torturous arm rebelled against him. The pain slivered all the way up his arm, into his shoulder and his chest. The cooling cocktail of shit and vomit seeped into the puckered wound on his ruined hand. His swollen elbow gave it all up as a bad job, and he flopped, face down into the grime puddle underneath him.

He exhaled.

Beige bubbles formed in the shit around his mouth, as the frothy filth began to seep into his mouth and up his nostrils.

Am I dying?

He thought he probably was.

He needed to get up, but the simple fact of the matter was, he couldn't move. His hand, his arm, his body, everything about him was just useless hulks. Everything was swollen, purple, and sickly warm. His stubbed fingers had drawn into a claw and were frozen in place, they refused to obey his brain's orders to move, not even to wiggle.

Panic flowed through him, and he tried to fill his lungs with air. All that happened was more shit, more vomit, more filth seeped into him. He couldn't swallow, he couldn't breathe. His face, his nostrils, his throat were all coated his own expulsions.

He gasped, swallowing more of the vile mixture.

His stomach flipped again, attempting to empty itself from both ends. Stinging liquid seemed to seep from everywhere, but mostly his bottom. The hot vomit had nowhere to go. It couldn't penetrate the blockage in his throat, in its hate to expel itself of the confines of his ravaged body.

Tears welled in the corners of his red eyes. They were the only clean things in the pit he now wallowed in.

They stung as they ran down the side of his face, leaving a clean stripe in their wake.

I don't want to die, he sobbed as his body began to buck beneath him, struggling for that elusive, life-giving air.

More cocktail poured into his gaping mouth and up his nose.

The world began to swim around him.

He thought of his father and his father's friends.

Memories swamped him.

He remembered what they'd done to him. He remembered their white stuff all over him as they laughed. He had opened his mouth back then and tasted it.

It tasted the same as the vomit and shit that encased him now.

It was not his finest memory.

~~~~

The world became darker, and he could feel the presence of someone lurking in the gloom around him. He was scared. He didn't like being alone, and whoever it was in the darkness refused to reveal themselves.

They were waiting for him to die.

'Who's there?' he whispered. He was amazed that he could talk, as his mouth had been so clogged with shit. But now he found he could breathe too, and he was no longer in his bed, he was no longer in his house.

'Who's there?' he asked again, buoyed by his newfound ability. 'Where am I?' he demanded.

A figure stepped out of the darkness.

It wasn't the same person who had died in her bed. It wasn't the same person he'd cut up with the electric knife. It wasn't the same person

126

he'd rubbed himself over with a cheese filled penis before eating her breasts.

Although, in a way, it was.

She was young. Her hair was long, dark, and wavy. She was beautiful. To him, she was the most beautiful thing he'd ever seen.

She no longer had the full figure of her middle-aged years, but she was blessed with the curvature and beauty, of youth.

'Mother?' he whispered. 'Is that you?'

She stepped into the light, and he saw her smile. She was nodding. 'My Gordon,' she whispered. It was only two words, but they were enough to fill his whole world, his entire existence.

He smiled.

She held out her arms.

He raised his own, accepting her embrace and was amazed to see they were the arms of a child, a baby.

He looked at her. Her hair was caught in a breeze he couldn't feel.

Not yet anyway.

He went to her. To his Andrea.

They embraced, and the breeze caressed him. As he hugged her, it became a wind. The feel of her in his child's arms was warm and alive.

It was so good.

She smelt wonderful, like something he hadn't smelt in what felt like a lifetime.

She smelt like flowers.

And cheese!

D E McCluskey

Zola

FULL DISCLOSURE, I hate this story.

I hate that this whole concept was developed in my brain. Yet, I love it too …

I felt for Andrea.

She had so many dreams and ambitions.

I loved poor Gordon. He was such a victim. First from an abusive father, then the environment his father put him in. Finally, he is victimised by his mother and her naivety, as she struggles to care for him.

And then I feel for me, as the writer, having to deal with these fucking vile demons, and the fact that I thought this whole thing up!

Originally, this was conceived as a Christmas comedy, where an obese boy eats so much cheese that he starts to become cheese, and then proceeds to eat himself (I still might write that, just to exorcise that particular demon). But it evolved into something meaner, something filthier, and something I hope my extreme horror readers will enjoy.

It is a tale of love, fear of the unknown, and a salute to the ingenuity of the human spirit in the face of adversity (what a crock of shit that is, it's a fucking book about cannibalism, and cheese).

It knocked me sick quite a few times as I wrote it, even more than when I wrote Cravings, although I believe that to be a more brutal tale.

I'm still not entirely comfortable writing extreme horror, it is not a genre I read too often, but what I have found is that it's loads of fun to let the grossness out every now and then, always pushing for that *something else* that might/will gross the readers out.

It is cathartic.

I have a few more extreme horror tales in me to make up the extreme series I'm committed to.

On that note, I'm off to start writing a new tale, one that is not vile, just to cleanse my brain for a few weeks.

Here are my acknowledgments …

First, I must, as always, acknowledge Tony Higginson, my long-time collaborator. I think he suffered in the proofreading of this nasty little book. Sorry, mate.

I want to put a big thank you in here to a modern horror hero. He might not be everyone's cup of tea, but in my earlier days, when I was just a fledgling author, creating graphic novels here and there, he gave me advice, and really helped me along the way. That thanks goes to Matt Shaw (or THE Matt Shaw as he likes to call himself). Thank you for the sterling pearls of wisdom, and for all the oral sex in the toilets in the comic cons. He told me *that* was the only way to thrive in this industry. I have gone through bottles and bottles of mouthwash since.

Next, the most excellent Lisa Lee Tone, my editor. Now, Lisa has edited most of my books, the vast majority being mainstream horror, with the odd nod to gore and the vile, here and there … The last book she edited for me was a children's book about seagulls. I think that was the real horror for her. She is a fan of the more extreme side of things, so Lisa, I've dedicated this book to you.

Normally I ask my sister to proofread, and Lauren, my long-suffering partner, but when they asked what this one was about (the title or the cover never gave anything away) I *had* to tell them. They both actively refused … and I can't say I blame them. They might never have looked at me the same again, and Christmas is only around the corner.

I had a team of five ARC readers I want to thank.

These guys are loyal readers, and not in the least bit afraid of a little bit of gore. So, a huge thank you to Corrina Morse, Christina Pfeiffer, Margaret Hammett, Renee Nieuwenhuyse, and R.E Shambrook (and a huge *sorry* too).

Lastly, I want to thank you, you sick, twisted, fun-loving reader of filth you. If it hadn't been for the love you showed Cravings, and CRACK, then this book, Gordon, Andrea, and Anthony would never have seen the light of day.

You sick bastards.

I love you all … Keep reading AND reviewing.

Dave McCluskey

Liverpool

October 2021

D E McCluskey

Other works by DE McCluskey

Cravings

The Special Stuff

The Stinky Stump

CRACK

The Boyfriend

The Twelve

And not forgetting:

Santa's Lost Book

(this one is for the kids)

Printed in Great Britain
by Amazon

59506979R00076